SHORT STORY COLLECTION

Volume III

ROBERT WILSON

PAGE PUBLISHING, INC.
Conneaut Lake, PA

First originally published by Page Publishing 2021

ISBN 978-1-6624-3035-0 (pbk)
ISBN 978-1-6624-3041-1 (digital)

Printed in the United States of America

CONTENTS

Robert has enjoyed writing these stories. His humor is in many of the stories. Some are sad; others have a happy ending. The results are up to the person reading his stories. Matti is funny; Jeana Poole is sad. Guss is—well, you decide. One lost man, sad but a good ending. Writing takes a lot of imagination to create a good story. Some stories Robert did in one afternoon. Others took several days to get the story in good form. Lana took several hours, and he liked the results.

Zelda is one tough woman. You will love reading about her. Robert spent two years writing these stories, and he still gets tears in his eyes reading them. He is sure you will too. Cry and laugh as you read his stories. Robert loves writing the short stories. The most excitement is finding another fictional person to write about. Some names were grabbed out of the air and find something to say about him or her. He gets a thrill to write a new story about anyone.

Many of the names are part of his classmates and people he met while in the navy.

ALLEN AND DELLA

Two young children go for a walk into the forest of central Idaho. It is early morning when these two realize they are lost. The boy, Allen, and the girl, Della, found themselves walking in circles. For hours the children were getting scared. The sun is setting in the west, and neither one knows how to find their way back home. The two are only nine years old. Not related to each other, just good school friends. Allen found a place to spend the night in a small rock shelter. This puts them out of the wind and rain.

Both are cold and shivering, but they stayed warm by holding each other. Nighttime comes. No light, no way to start a fire. Neither one knew how to start one, even if they had the right things. Allen and Della lay down and fell to sleep. Allen heard growling, he sat up and looked around. In the moonlight, Della saw several sets of eyes. She started crying because she knew what those eyes were. A pack of wolves was within attacking range.

A strange voice was heard off in the distance. The wolf pack took off running away from the two children. The voice came closer, then a torchlight came in view. "Whoever it is, maybe we have been found," Della said.

A few minutes later, a big man came into view. Allen and Della stood up. The man said, "What are you two doing this far away from home?"

Allen said, "We went for a walk and got lost."

"You are thirty miles from any towns."

"How do we get home, mister?"

"Not tonight. Follow me, and you can stay at my house tonight."

The morning came, and the children found something for breakfast. The old man was nowhere to be found. The house looked like it hadn't been lived in for a hundred years. The house was made of logs with a potbelly stove for heat. A cookstove was also in the house.

Back home, there was a large search party looking for the two missing children. Two days, a week, and then a month. No sign of the children. Allen and Della stayed in the house. Neither one of them knew which way to go. The search party continued for six months. Finally, the searching came to an end. Everyone in town set up a memorial for the two children. In memory of Allen Davis and Della Hardy.

Allen learned how to start a fire. Della cleaned up their house the best a nine-year-old could do. Allen went out looking for something to eat. He found some berries and an apple tree. He looked around and saw that he was in an orchard. He made a trail to the house so he would not get lost. Della helped gather some apples and lots of berries. Meat was needed to help them stay strong and alive.

Allen found some spears in a room in the house and a home-made bow. He was not strong enough to pull the string back, so he just used the arrows like small spears. The spears were in good shape. Allen carried a spear, and Della was carrying three arrows. A rabbit was their first kill. Della stabbed it with an arrow. "Good work, Della, but we need more meat. Our apples and berries are all gone."

Allen started a fire in the woodburning cookstove and helped Della skin out the rabbit. Della was learning how to cook. She only burned one side of the rabbit. The whole rabbit was eaten. They couldn't afford to waste anything. The next morning, Allen went out to the orchard. There was a small deer eating some grass. Allen sneaked up as close as possible.

Twenty feet away, the deer heard him and started to leave. He threw the spear. The spear hit the deer in the middle stomach. The spear fell out, and the deer continued to run for a few more yards. He fell down, and Allen stabbed the deer again in the neck cutting his throat. The wolf pack came around. Allen stabbed at several wolves. The pack moved back.

Allen used his spear to open up the deer and pulled out the inner parts.

He pulled the rest of the deer back to the house, and Della helped skin out the deer.

Three rabbits and two squirrels—Della was learning to cook without burning their food. Now this deer would last for a while. There wasn't a refrigerator, so some of it would go to waste. That man showed up for a couple of hours. He showed the kids how to save all the deer meat by drying it. He vanished again. The deer meat would be enough to get them through the winter.

Snow started falling. Both kids went out to gather as much firewood as they could before it got buried under the snow. The meat was all dried and put away. The mice and rats could not get to the meat. More firewood will be needed because the snow was getting deeper. Della asked, "When will the snow stop falling? I want to go home." She started crying. Allen held her and started crying also.

He stopped crying and said, "We have to be strong, Della." She stood up and went to the bed and lay down. She was asleep in five minutes. Allen went outside looking for more firewood. The snow quit falling for a while. He found some limbs that fell from the weight of the snow. He brought in what he could find.

The shed by the back of the house had not been looked at by either one of the kids. Allen took the wood in and went back out to the shed. He had to move some snow to open the door. Looking inside, he found a gold mine of things he could use. Some animal traps, an ax, a shovel, and a big stack of firewood. On a counter, there were three knives and some old fruit jars. Nothing was in them.

He loaded up his arms and then stopped. Hanging on the wall next to the door was a sled. He dropped the wood and got the sled down, loaded it up with wood, and pulled it into the house. Della was awake now. She got a big smile on her face when she saw all that firewood. "Where did you find all that wood?"

"In that shed in the trees behind the house. There is much more wood in the shed, plus an ax, a shovel, and I found these knives." She went to Allen and gave him a kiss. "I love you, Allen." She put two pieces in the potbelly stove. The house warmed up real quick. Two happy and warm children. A handful of dried venison deer meat—both sat down and ate lunch.

Allen went back to the shed with the sleigh. Della rode on the sled.

Together, the shed was searched for anything that could be used to help them get through the winter. Another load of wood then back to the house with more firewood. Allen went outside looking for something to eat other than dried deer meat. He had two spears. He saw a rabbit, moved closer to the rabbit, then he heard a growl behind him.

A mountain lion was within striking distance. The lion jumped at Allen. All he could do was to point the spears at the big cat. He raised the spears a little. Both spears went through the lion's chest, killing him. Allen lay under the lion for a couple of minutes then rolled it off him. He was still shaking. After another couple of minutes, he took a knife and opened up the cat. He removed the insides but kept the heart.

The cat weighed over three times his weight, but he did manage to drag the lion home. Della looked out the window and saw Allen dragging something. She wrapped up and went outside to help him get his kill into the house. Della asked, "What does cat meat taste like?"

"I don't know. I guess we will find out." Allen cut some pieces off, and Della cleaned the frying pan and cooked some strips of the cat. The lion meat had a different taste, but it wasn't bad. The deer skin made a wrap for Allen when he went outside.

The lion skin was cleaned, and Della said, "I want this skin when I have to go out." Allen said okay.

The cat meat was cut up into some steaks and cooked. The rest was hung outside. He said, "This is our refrigerator." Then he laughed. The temperature was cold enough to freeze anything if left outside for any length of time. Four months in the snow and the weather was starting to warm up. Still plenty of snow on the ground, the small animals were out and looking for something to eat. Allen was also. He killed three more rabbits.

The total was nine rabbit skins. Now Della could make herself some warm shoes. Allen helped scrape the skins. Della boiled the skins to rid them of bugs. The rabbit meat, some cooked, and the rest was put out in the freezer. The weather was still cold. The cat meat gave them diarrhea, so no more of it was eaten. The only food they had was the rabbits.

Both of them went outside. The sunshine felt good on their bodies.

"Which way is home?" Della asked. They had been lost in the woods for nine months now.

A voice from nowhere said, "Go downhill." The old man was there again.

"Sir, who are you?" Allen asked.

"Adam." Then the man disappeared into the woods.

Allen and Della went back to the house, put out the fires, and got a spear and knife each and what other food that was still good to eat. They kept the animal skins 'cause the weather was not very warm. Allen asked Della, "Do you want to leave here now or stay for a while longer?" She wrapped her arms around him and said, "I love you, but I want to see my parents again."

"I do too. I want to see mine again."

There was plenty of daylight left. Allen pointed, and they started walking downhill. Five hours had passed when he was looking at a logging road. Della followed Allen onto the road and headed downhill on the road. About an hour going down the road, a truck came up the road. The driver stopped and looked at the two children in amazement.

The driver turned the truck around and headed back to town with the two children in the truck. One of the loggers called the sheriff. When the truck got back to town, the whole town was waiting for the two lost children. Their parents were waiting for them to arrive home. The truck drove into town, and everyone was anticipating the sight of two missing children for over nine months.

The truck had to stop because the crowd was blocking the street. One of the mothers screamed. The crowd dispersed and let the parents get to the truck. Everyone went totally quiet waiting for the parents to see their children. Tears flowed from all eyes as the parents held their children. The children and parents went to the police station. There the chief talked to the children separately. Their words were the same.

Allen said, "We went for a walk and got lost. We ended walking in circles, I guess. This man found us and we went to his house. We were cold and wet."

"Were you kidnapped?"

"No, Dad, we were lost."

The sheriff asked, "What did he look like?"

"I don't know. It was dark, and all we wanted was to find a warm place to stay."

His mom asked, "Did he stay there with you?"

"No. We didn't see him again for a long time. We only saw him a couple of times. He showed us how to make the food last a long time by drying it over the hot stove. Then he was gone again."

The sheriff asked, "Who killed the deer and mountain lion?"

"I did with the spears. The deer was easy. The mountain lion jumped at me. I pointed the spears at him and he landed on them."

"I don't believe you. That story is a bunch of crap." Allen's dad got up and hit the sheriff knocking him off his chair. "Don't you ever call my son a liar. You were not there."

The sheriff got up and told his deputy to lock him up. "No. You were out of line with your remarks." The sheriff went outside.

The deputy asked, "When was the last time you saw this man?"

"The weather was getting warmer. The snow was melting. We were outside and trying to guess which way to our home." Allan took a drink of water. "The man appeared again and said, 'Go downhill.' Della asked his name. He said Adam."

Everyone gasped. The deputy said, "Other people had meetings with Adam over the past fifty years. Some spent a night or two in his house. No one could find his house again. All that was left of the house was a pile of rubble where the house used to be."

Dad got tears in his eyes. "Son, Adam died over a hundred years ago. You and Della spent the winter with the most famous Spirit in the state. Allen's story and Della's story were almost the same. Nothing was left out. Nobody could deny that their stories were not true. The sheriff had a shiner. He earned it.

His mom held him. "No more long walks son." She cried again. He and Della went to their homes. The two families lived next door to each other. April was here, and neither one wanted to go to school. The kids missed too much to get a passing grade. Their parents said, "We will let them start over come next September."

Allen's dad checked the state records and found that Adam was a military veteran. He died after returning from the civil war. He homesteaded that area. One square mile. His name was Adam Johanson. He was a very gentle man. His wife died before he returned home from fighting during the civil war. He left his home in town and moved up to the woods.

Allen and Della celebrated their tenth birthdays together: Della, June 22, and Allen, June 30. Their parents started teaching their children what they missed while gone from home. Allen's mom borrowed some books from the school. English, math and history. Their mothers spent almost every day teaching their two children. The moms wanted them to catch up with their original class. Hopefully, Allen and Della could rejoin their classmates.

Della was doing better than Allen but not that much better. Both kids wanted to get back with their class, so the two put their all in the studying. Three months with their noses in the books and now ready to take some tests from the teachers. The two were separated—two different rooms—and went through several tests each. Both of them passed every test and were advanced to the fifth grade. Allen and Della were very happy.

September was here, and the two went back to their original class.

All the students welcomed them back. Their teacher said, "We are here together to learn some new things. I do not want to hear a thousand questions to Allen and Della. Those two children have been grilled before, so give them a break." They were left alone. The year went well. Allen and Della spent a lot of time together after school was out for the day.

The two really cared for each other. After spending nine months together in the wild woods, their minds were working together without seeing the other one. They loved each other. The next three years went by fast, and then high school. Now fourteen and ready to start a different way of schooling, the two were spending more time away from the other students.

Allen and Della were reading more books on how to survive in the wilderness. Together the two were thinking about going back to the wilderness and surviving after graduation. The two had sneaked off many times in the last three years and made love. "We can survive out there," Allen said. "I love you, honey. Do you want to go with me or stay here?"

"I love you too, baby. Yes, I am ready to go now, but we have three more months before graduation."

"Can you wait that long, honey?"

"Yes, I will wait, but what will we tell our parents?"

"I have no idea. I won't lie to them. Maybe just tell them what our plans are."

Della said, "They will not agree with our plans."

"Do you really care?"

"Yes. I want them on our side. We can let them know what is on our minds, and if it doesn't work out the way we plan, then we can come home and find a job."

"In this small town? There is nothing to look forward to. This is just a deadbeat town. If you don't get perfect grades all four years, you will never get out of this town."

"I know you are right, sweetie, but crap, are you ready to leave now?"

"Let's graduate first."

"Okay, if you say so." The day finally came, and Allen and Della graduated. Two very happy young adults. The two relaxed for a week then got their parents together for a celebration.

Allen started talking first. "Mom, Dad, we love each other. We find that there are no jobs in town. We want to move to Adam's property."

Then all hell broke out. All four parents protested. "You two are crazy. You will not survive there alone."

Della said, "Dad, Mom, we survived nine months with little help. Adam only showed us a few things. The rest was up to us. We can build a house for ourselves."

Allen said, "We have been reading many books on survival. We are young and willing to give life in the woods a try. I have a compass this time."

Della said, "And we have maps of this country. If we die, we will send you a letter."

"Quit trying to be funny, girl. I am not impressed," her father said.

Della said, "I love you both very much. Our minds are not on the same pace. We want to try life in the wild."

Allen said, "We have more experience and more things available to us. I can string a bow, use a spear, and start a fire with the two right rocks."

"I can cook without burning our food." Allen laughed.

She hit him playfully. "Honey."

Allen said, "Let us try. If we fail, we will let you know where we are. We will come home and find a job of some kind. Please, Mom, Dad."

His dad said, "I will give you...will we see you two for Christmas?"

Mom said, "Please, son. We love you."

"I love you too, Mom, Dad."

Della said, "Mom, Dad, can we try our dreams? We are not children any more. We respect you, but we are older than before."

Finally, their parents said, "Okay, but you must contact us if you run into any trouble."

Della's father gave Allen a 30-06 with fifty rounds of ammunition. "Take good care of this rifle. It will keep you alive."

"Thank you, sir. I will."

Allen's father bought a nine-millimeter pistol and gave it to them. He added fifty rounds with the pistol. Both of them were taken to the local gun range for some practice. The broad side of the barn was too far away. After more practice, their target was within sight. Now that both of them were better with the two weapons. Their parents felt a little better.

Allen and Della packed up some gear and headed up to the wilderness camp. They had their animal skins, rabbit shoes, a rifle, and pistol. A large pack of food that was a week of supply. The compass took them close to where Adam's house was. With an ax and several knives, the two set up camp with a tent and a fire to keep the wild animals away. The next morning, Allen led the way to where Adam's house used to be.

Della said, "This is it. We are there." She was looking at a pile of rotten logs. "Can we rebuild his home?"

Allen said, "All we can do is try. The winter is not far away, so we will get us a shelter first and work on the house later." Allen started building a shelter for Della and himself. After two weeks, their shelter was rain- and snow-proof. A very strong shelter. He had a saw to cut down trees for a new house.

The cutting lasted for several months. The snow stopped their building but did not deter their ambition. The two kept on working in the snow and added two layers to a new house. Their fireplace kept them warm. It was almost a cave and not far from the original Adam house. The new house would be about fifty yards from Adam's property.

Allen took a break and went hunting.

Two rabbits killed with the bow and a big buck, also with the bow.

Their cave was kept warm with plenty of firewood, which kept the wild animals away. Neither one wanted to kill a mountain lion. Their meat tasted terrible. Neither one wanted diarrhea again. Fortunately, neither one ran into a mountain lion. Rabbit and deer. The building continued until the weather got too bad for them to work anymore.

Their camp was well-protected from the rain and snow. Plenty of firewood was stored before the snow started falling. Just hope it was enough to last through the winter. Allen went out and gathered much more firewood. He wanted to make sure they had enough to get them through the winter. The air was getting much colder, but the enclosed shelter was the best the two had ever built.

With an abundance of firewood, the winter was not a problem.

Several months passed, and the two had a baby on the way. Only a month away. On February 4, a little girl was born. Allen and Della hand-delivered a letter to their parents. "We thought you would like to meet your granddaughter. Their parents were so happy.

Della's mother asked, "Who delivered the baby?"

"Allen did. He helps me with everything. Isn't she beautiful?"

The parents were so happy they couldn't say much of anything.

Della and Allen went back to their cave and continued building their new house. All summer, the house went up. The last logs for the house went up. Now the roof was the next project.

Allen and Della's fathers came up and helped them put on a roof. Allen and Della did not turn away their help. They were so happy for the assistance in getting the roof on their house. Their mothers showed up a week later with two little babies.

"Mom, oh my goodness, he is so beautiful," Allen said.

Della asked, "Is that my little brother?"

Her mother had a great sense of humor. "No, I found him on the street and kept him. Yes, honey." Her dad laughed. Mom said, "You are not the only one that can have a baby. Did you know that the pioneers had twelve to fifteen children? How many will you have?"

"Mom, not that many." The families had a good reunion. After the roof was done, their parents left and went back to the dead town. Their parents knew it and started looking for something better. Their parents listened to their children. Those children are well-versed on the future.

Allen's parents, Jim and Sally, found better jobs in Lewiston, and Della's parents, Janet and Benjamin, went to Boise. There her dad landed a good job working in automotive repair. Her mother started working as a nurse in a hospital.

Allen and Della went back to their house up in the wilderness. This was their home. Neither one saw Adam again. We guessed that his soul went to rest in heaven. He was such a good man. It was such a shame that he was gone, but nobody lives forever. Allen went to the orchard. It wasn't regular hunting season, but Allen didn't care. Food was needed. He had to go out and find it.

Allen killed six rabbits and seven mink. The rabbits and mink would make great clothing parts and good food. He was waiting for hunting season. Both Allen and Della went to town to get a legal hunting license and deer tags for their area. The licenses were granted to both of them. Allen knew where the deer would be every day and night. With only one rifle, Allen would be with Della when she was hunting. Their baby was with them. Their limit was two bucks and two does.

Their take for the year was three deer. One buck got away. The meat was put in a smoker. The meat tasted better smoked than dried.

Della was spending most of her time taking care of their baby girl, Becky.

She was a growing little baby. At one year old, she was an active baby. That was a good sign. Their parents were very happy for Becky's activity.

Allen went to the orchard and picked a few boxes of apples and brought them back to their new house. Several days to clean and can them for future use. Apples and berries were placed in fruit jars and canned for the winter food supply. We had modern equipment to take care of our winter food supply. We were almost ready for winter. We had soft rabbit shoes, deer skins for clothes, and good blankets for our beds. What else did we need?

The winter was upon us. It got well digger cold. We stayed inside as long as we could. Allen went out to get more firewood when the snow quit falling. There were many trees that had fallen from age. Those trees were dead. Allen was able to drag some of them back to where he could cut them up with a power saw. This was their firewood for the winter. They had enough firewood and food.

Allen and Della plus Becky could make it through their second winter with the needs fulfilled. Allen and Della lived well through the winter. Their little girl was very happy. She stayed inside with one of her parents watching over her. March came. The sun came out, and everyone was happier. Allen went looking for more food. There was a small lake close so Allen went to see if he could spear some fish.

With no fishing pole, he used arrows and spears. He managed to get several fish, enough to last two days. Maybe by then he could get some other food type. The rabbits were out looking for pasture grass; beavers were looking for saplings for food and dam building. Allen was looking for anything that moved. One rabbit was all he got. Not much, just one meal. Della said, "I think it's time to go home."

"I agree with you. We can be home in five hours. If we leave now, we can be home before dark. It is only four miles to the logging road, then down to the truck stop for our vehicle."

"Let me wrap Becky and get going."

"I can come back and get everything later." Their trip to the truck stop was a long walk, but they were happy to be there. Allen went in the office and retrieved the car keys. On their way home now, the two felt a great relief. Allen said, "No more ventures into the wild."

Della said, "I agree, but now what are we going to do?"

"Find a job and start thinking about how to pay for college."

Della said, "We can live in my grandparents house and attend the local college. Idaho Falls is a big city." Their plans were working but real slow.

Allen said, "I want you to go to college first. I will continue working. Don't argue with me."

Della smiled. "Okay."

Allen went back to the wilderness house, brought back the important things, and put a sign on the door:

Use but clean up your mess.
—Adam's friend

Now back in Idaho Falls, Allen continued working while Della was in school. She wanted a degree in finance. Allen was taking night classes at the junior college. Becky celebrated her second birthday. She was growing fast. Allen wanted to be a machinist. His classes were on machine shop training, the use of all types of machines.

Allen was enjoying his classes. The first year, he learned how to use four different types of machines.

Della was doing great with her classes. Her GPA was 3.71. She was in the top five of the class at the end of her first year. She got a summer job and saved every penny for the next year. A finance company looked at the students taking finance classes. Della wasn't the top student, but grades were not everything. Sharpness and attitude. She was asked to come to their office for an interview. She thought, *What is this for?* She showed up at the office and wondering why was she called there.

The secretary asked, "Are you Della?"

"Yes, I am. Why am I here?"

"Have a seat please." She made a call.

A man came out. "I am Gary." He shook her hand. "Come with me." She followed him to a conference room. There were two other people in the room. She sat down, and then the questions started coming. She answered every question with a positive attitude. The three people, two men and a woman, looked at each other.

The woman said, "Thank you Della. Would you go out to the secretary and have a seat?"

Della went to the front and sat down. A few minutes later, the company president came out and sat down by her.

The woman came out and said, "We are looking for a well-qualified person. You are very intelligent, but you need more schooling." Her heart fell to her stomach. "Don't feel bad because we will pay for your schooling for the remaining three years, okay?"

She jumped up and gave the woman a hug then said, "I'm sorry."

"Don't be, just keep doing what you are doing in school. I will set up your scholarship in a few days." The secretary printed off several papers, and Della read them and signed in the required places. "These two are for you. Take them to the college and present them to the scholarship office later this month. The rest of your classes will be paid for you." She had tears in her eyes. "Thank you all very much."

"Will you want to work here after graduation? We hope you will."

"Yes, I will. I will be back in three years."

"How about summer work here?" the vice president said.

"A job now?"

"Why not. On-the-job training. It will help you through school."

The woman said, "Follow me, and I will show you to your desk."

Della got home and was so excited she started crying. Becky said, "Mama, don't cry."

"Honey, these are happy tears."

Allen asked, "What happened, baby?"

"I got a summer job working for the finance company, and the company is paying for my remaining three years of schooling."

BILL WILSON

A young man just finishing high school and looking for a college degree. He spent two years in junior college then joined his brothers in the Navy. Now all four of them were in the military, he excelled fast to make E-6. In Vietnam with two other brothers, Bill was well-respected by his peers. The war ended, and Bill went to several types of ships. After nine years, Bill made chief. Several years later, the two older brothers retired, Bill stayed for a few years, and retired after thirty years as a master chief.

That was not the end of his namesake. Bill passed away shortly after his retirement. The next older brother had a house in Ogdon, Utah. Another Bill Wilson found that house, and it was up for sale. He had enough money to purchase the house. Bill had sense remarried. His new wife had been married to a rich man that died from cancer. She was five years older than Bill.

Bill was happy for a while until his new wife passed away. Bill didn't know what she was worth. That didn't matter because he had just lost his second wife. *Why is life so cruel to me?* he thought. Several days and weeks passed. He didn't want to get to close to anyone. Maybe that person might die. After several months, he met a young woman, Alice, and asked her out for dinner. She accepted.

The two spent many happy times together. The couple was happy. Bill proposed to her. She accepted his proposal. The two were married three weeks later, and she moved into his house with him. Over the next six years, Alice had two children. She left a short while later. She went back to Twin Falls, Idaho. The divorce was filed, and Bill was free but lonely again.

Bill met another young woman. She was beautiful. Bill took her out for dinner several times. She was very interested in Bill. She was trying to get through college. Donna was working to get through her third year of college. The two were married a week later. The first year together, Donna was pregnant. She finished her college with Bill's help. Over five years, Donna had three children. Her fourth and last pregnancy, Donna had twins. She was thirty-nine now with a flock of children. Two very happy people. Their family was growing up fast. Their children, David, Jeani, Jennifer, and the twins, Gary and Terri.

Bill thought the curse was over. He had beaten it. Bill was six feet tall. His oldest son grew to six feet two inches. Their two daughters reached five feet ten inches at the age of fourteen. David graduated from high school with one sister a year behind him and the third, two years back. The twins were two years behind the youngest sister. Eleven years earlier, Bill had received five million dollars from his second wife's will. He was totally surprised.

His third wife knew nothing about his fortune from his second wife. He had moved most of it to a fidelity account. That account grew fast. David had a girlfriend, Sally, but she could only afford one semester at a time. Bill purchased a two-bedroom house close to Weber State. He was hoping all their children would go to college. Dave invited her to move into the house and finish college with him. She accepted. Now she didn't have to work as much. Just one full-time job during the summer and part time while school was going on.

Bill had a mechanical engineering degree he had received during his time in college. With the money from his late wife, he didn't have to work. Donna was unhappy being married. She said, "I want a divorce. Since we have been married, all we do is fight. I love you, sweetie, but I cannot live in a fighting home." Bill cried, and the two divorced.

Things were better now. Both of them were happy and still living together. Donna met a struggling student. She had dropped out twice to work and save enough money for another semester of college. Donna said to Cathy, "Come home with me and stay here to finish college."

Bill said, "That will be okay with me. Your room will be across the hall from our room." The children were sleeping downstairs. Donna finished her college and was now a teacher. She was teaching the fourth grade at the new school for Shadow Valley children and some of the out-of-boundary kids. The school needed thirty children in each class. Cathy had two children, Steve and Sue, with a lazy ex-husband she had left three years earlier.

Cathy said, "Thank you, Donna and Bill. I can work for this room and help pay for the food we eat."

Bill said, "Just graduate, then we will talk about the expenses." She gave both of them a hug with tears in her eyes. Her children were staying downstairs with Donna's children. One area for the girls and another room for the boys. Another school year started, and all the kids were in school with Donna. Cathy was still at home. Her first class didn't start for another hour.

Bill thought she was gone. He went down the hall in his birthday suit. Cathy walked out of her room at the same time. Both stopped and looked at each other. Bill invited her to his room. Cathy missed her first class of the day. She left for the second class very satisfied and happy. The day ended for everyone. The children went to their rooms and did their homework, then Donna turned on the downstairs TV.

She and Bill went out back and talked with Cathy. Cathy was ready to leave. Donna said, "No, you don't have to leave. We are not married anymore. Was it good?"

Cathy smiled and said, "I have never been that happy in my life, yes." Over the next three years, Cathy completed her college degree as a teacher. Several times each month, the three would be sleeping in the same bed when morning came. During that time, Cathy gave birth to two girls. Donna also had another child. A very handsome boy. He named their son, Robert Lee Wilson.

Bill knew his life was coming to an end but told no one. He went to the Internet searching for his son's name. He knew he had a twin brother. His adopted mother told him just before she died. She told Bill his brother's name. He went through all the Robert Wilsons and found his twin brother in Missouri. The birth date and name plus size matched. Bill made out his will to include Robert Lee Wilson, with his Missouri address.

Bill talked to Donna and Cathy what he was told and what he found. "My life is short, honey. I love you both. Bring him here to replace me." The three cried for a few minutes. Bill died two weeks after finishing his will. The funeral and cremation were held without little Robert knowing what happened to his father. Three weeks had passed when Bill's lawyer finally found Robert.

The lawyer, Jim James, said, "You have a family in Utah."

"My family is here in Missouri." The lawyer talked to Robert for several hours, and Rob said, "What if I don't go?"

"You will lose seven million dollars and a son and two wives that miss you very much. You look just like your twin brother. Your son is waiting for you to come home, Robert." A pause. "He is almost two years old. Your wives are Donna and Cathy. You married both of them then divorced them."

"Shit. I cannot fathom being married and divorced to someone I have never met." He laughed. "I have already been married and divorced three times, but I didn't stay with them after the divorce. Okay, what is the address I have to go to?" He was told the address and signed some papers. "I built up that house many years ago. What does it look like now?"

"When you get there, you will know."

Robert packed up some clothes and other things then drove to Ogden, Utah, went to the address, and walked up the back steps. The same ones he had put in the ground twenty-five years earlier. He reached the top, and a little man came running to him. "Daddy, Daddy, you are home."

Robert held his new son, Robert Junior, RJ. "Daddy, don't stay gone so long anymore. I miss you, Daddy." He was crying.

Rob held RJ and walked to the two women sitting on the back porch. Both of them got up and walked to him and gave him a kiss. He put RJ down and held the two women. Each of them whispered to him their names then said, "We will talk later." Robert held RJ for a while, then his mom, Donna, put him to bed.

Robert and Donna and Cathy sat out back with a drink of bourbon and water. Donna and Cathy talked to Robert for a few hours telling him what happened and why RJ didn't know his father had died. "You are now his father, please, honey. He needs you."

Cathy said, "We need you too, sweetie." She smiled.

"You have me for several years, honey. Both of you. Just give me some time to get used to this much affection." Everyone laughed. Donna's and Cathy's children knew that Bill died. Their children were much older. No one told RJ. He thinks Robert is his father. He was almost two when Bill died. Donna's youngest two, the twins, went into the Navy.

Donna was fifty-five, and Cathy was fifty-one now. All the children were now out of school except for Robert Jr. He would start school in a couple of years. Robert was seventy-four. He was still able to satisfy his two new ex-wives. The lawyer came by to make sure Robert had kept his promise when he signed the papers. The bank accounts, checking and savings, and fidelity accounts were transferred to Robert Lee Wilson Sr.

Robert called his oldest sister. He asked her, "What do you know about me and a twin brother? Don't lie to me, Rose. I need to know the truth."

"Honey, I don't know everything, but when you were born, our mom said there was a second baby born also. Mom told me many years later that she could not handle twins, so she gave Bill to your dad's brother. Did you find him?"

"No, he found me." He started crying. "But he died a month ago. I never got to meet him face-to-face, but I am here with his ex-wives and son that thinks I am his father. I am not going to let him down." Rob was almost crying again.

"Honey, I am sorry things turned out the way they did. I never met your brother either. I totally forgot about him. Where are you now?"

"Back in Utah in the same house that I spent most of my retirement money on. My twin brother bought it, and now I own it according to his will. I had thought about going back to Utah, and now I am here and very happy."

Rose said, "I am sorry you didn't know about your twin brother earlier. That is all I can say."

"Rose, how is your rental home doing?"

"I had to sell it. I was not making any money. Not even enough to pay the bills."

"Do you need any funding for anything?"

"No, honey. I am getting by. I have a few dollars after my bills are paid." Robert sent Rose twenty-five thousand dollars.

Robert asked, "Summer is almost here. Are you interested to look for any geodes?"

"No, honey. I am past the digging in the dirt for them." Summer vacation was here, and Robert called Jack. "Do you like it there, Jack?"

"No. Betty passed away last week. Her sister gave me two days to get out."

"Tell her to go to hell. The law will give you a month to get out. Check with the police department." A pause. "Come up here to Utah. I will find a house for you." A week later, Jack pulled up out front of Robert's house with a trailer loaded to the top. Rob walked out to meet him. He gave him a hug and asked, "What did you leave behind?"

The two laughed, and Jack said, "The trailer and the dirt on the driveway." More laughter.

Rob said, "I will get my truck, and you can follow me to your house. It is not far." Donna and Cathy locked up the house and went with Rob and RJ. The four of them got Jack unloaded in just a short time. The house was just below the new high school. It has been open for a year now. Cathy was teaching English in that school. Donna is teaching the fourth grade in the elementary school.

Rob gave Jack fifty thousand dollars. "Come summertime, we will be going to California and dig for some geodes."

Jack said, "I will pass for now. How much does it snow here?"

Donna said, "It gets deep. Are you allergic to snow?" We laughed.

"No, what will I need to dig myself out of the snow?"

Cathy said, "Try a snow shovel."

Monday morning came, and the teachers went back to school. RJ would start school in two more years. The weather was getting colder. Jack put Utah plates on his truck and went shopping for more food. He got everything in his truck and got in.

This woman came to him and asked, "Are you single?"

"Yes, I am."

"Do you want a housekeeper? I am homeless, cold, and hungry." She was almost crying. Jack got out and took her around to the other side and opened the door for her. He helped her in, closed the door, and got back in and drove home.

"Thank you, sir. My name is Shannon."

"I am Jack, and you are very welcome, Shannon." After getting all the food in the house, he showed her where she will be sleeping. She made her bed and went to the living room and sat by the heater beside Jack.

"I lost my husband in a divorce. I also got booted out of his house with very little clothing and less money. He left Utah for the sunny south. He sold the house and kept all of the money."

"I appreciate the company of a young woman. I will not kick you out. I am hungry. What would you like to eat?" Shannon cooked a steak; Jack cut up some things for a salad, and set the table with two glasses of wine.

Robert got a call from Norma. "My mom passed away this morning." She was crying.

"I am so sorry, Norma. I will come down there tomorrow." Rob called Donna and Cathy. He told them what happened and said, "I want to go to Arizona for a couple of days. Should I take RJ with me?"

Donna said, "No, I will watch him He does not need to be around a funeral."

Norma called back. "Robert, you don't need to come down. She will be cremated in two days."

"If that is what you want to do, then I will stay here." Robert sent Norma fifty-thousand-dollar check and a sympathy card.

She said, "Thank you very much, Uncle Robert. This will pay off my house with what Mom gave me."

Rob said, "You are very welcome, Norma."

Cathy talked to Robert and Donna. "My parents are not doing well. I have to go take care of them. I don't know when I will be back."

Robert said, "Take your time, honey. You will have a home here."

Robert, Donna, and their son plus Jack and pregnant Shannon headed for the geode beds in southern California. Rob stopped in Arizona and visited with Norma Webb. She gave Robert a hug. "I am debt-free, Uncle. Thank you very much." She held Rob for a minute. "Sorry, Donna. I love my uncle and your husband."

"I understand. Don't worry, I won't hurt you."

"Uncle Robert, do you want your sister's Jeep? I don't have a need for it."

Jack said, "May I have it, Norma? My truck is only a two-wheel drive. I had trouble getting around last winter."

Donna said, "I can use it. My little car got stuck many times last winter." Norma signed the title over to Donna and gave her the keys. We continued our trip to the geode beds in southern California. Once we got out of Arizona, she gave the keys to Jack. Robert found the road to the geode beds. He stopped before he got there.

He said, "Dig in the sandy areas around here." Everyone looked at him but started digging. A few minutes, Donna and Shannon started finding small geodes.

Donna said, "How did you know these were here?"

"Just lucky, I guess." He laughed. He told them about the man and his venture then got run off by the state for over staying his permit. They found close to seventy small geodes. They stopped there for the night and went on to the good beds not far away when the sun came up.

Jack really liked the jeep, but Donna would be getting it once we are back in Utah. We arrived to the area Robert wanted to dig in. The ditch was too much for his truck, so Jack drove the jeep to the geode bed. Rob and Donna with Robert Jr. walked to the beds. Only a few yards away.

Rob said, "Dang, someone got that big geode." He pointed to the spot it used to be.

Jack asked, "How big was it?"

"Maybe four feet in diameter. Huge, but there are more up here on that hillside." The digging. five sets of hands digging with a small rake.

The small geodes started showing up with some digging. We took a break for lunch and water. After eating, we went back to some more digging. Robert Jr. stopped and sat in the jeep. He fell asleep. Donna sat with him for a while. Jack and Rob continued digging. We went to the lower area.

After resting a few minutes, Jack said, "What is that bright thing shinning in my eyes?" He went up to the spot and dug a little bit and brought it out of the dirt. It was some white crystal with specks of gold. He dug deeper and found more crystal.

Robert helped him dig to find the full size of the crystal. The whole piece was close to two feet in diameter. We carried it down the hill and went through the ditch and put it in the pickup bed. We went back to the lower part of the hill and started finding some larger geodes. Some were eight to ten inches in diameter.

Donna and Shannon went to the other side of the hill. About ten minutes we heard a scream. Jack and Rob went to the top of the hill and saw the women digging out a large geode. Close to three feet in diameter. Robert moved the truck to the far side and backed up the truck, lowered the tail gate. The big geode was rolled down the hill and rolled it onto the pickup bed. Rob moved the Jeep to the other side.

RJ was sweating. Robert moved RJ into some shade and then put him in the front seat of the jeep and turned on the air-conditioning unit. We watched him closely. RJ was sitting up now and feeling better. Donna sat with him for a few minutes, then he wanted to do some more digging. RJ came out and helped Dad dig. The two found another big geode. Close to eighteen inches in diameter.

Everyone was tired, so we left there and went back to the camp ground for the night. The next morning, we went back to the dig area and found eleven big geodes from ten to fifteen inches.

Jack said, "Robert, time to quit." We all said yes.

Rob said, "There is one more place I want to visit," pointing to the west. In a half hour, we arrived at the area. "I have ten acres here. I see stakes in the ground. Someone has marked off their property. Jack, park here by this stake." Rob reset the mileage to zero checked the direction with a compass. Go that way for one half mile and stop." The front of the Jeep stopped by the second stake.

"Perfect. Robert checked the distance to the western stake. 220 yards. My ten-acre property starts right here. 220 yards west, 220 yards north. Robert used his range scope with jacks help. He piled rocks up to mark his property boundary. Two stakes were already in place."

A pickup came in to the area. The man said, "Your jeep is on my property." He was smiling.

Robert said, "That property west of your place is my ten acres."

"My name is James Townson. Do you want to sell your place?"

"Not just yet. I want to know what is under the ground on this property. I have had several offers up to thirty thousand dollars in the last five years."

James said, "Now I am not alone. Do you want to do some digging? I brought my back hoe. I want to see what is down there also." He spent digging about twenty feet with nothing.

Robert said, "I bet it is oil down there." He smiled. "Ask for one million dollars. If those people agree, it is oil."

RJ said, "Dad, what is this?" He was holding an almost clear rock. We all looked at it.

Jim said, "Oh my god. This is an uncut diamond." *Wow* was the noise from everyone.

His wife said, "Don't sell, honey." Jack got his rake from the truck and started raking Jim's diggings. An hour passed and sixty-three pieces of diamonds were found.

Robert asked, "Jim, would you mind digging here for a few minutes?"

"Not at all. Where do you want me to start?" Jim's diamonds we guessed at about sixty thousand dollars. Jim dug a big hole for us then stopped. "Thank you, Jim." We raked through the rocks. We found several small diamond pieces. Rob filled several buckets full of chocolate rock, while Donna and Shannon were looking for more diamonds. Jack was tired and quit looking for anything.

Finally, he got up and went through a pile of rocks. He dipped some rocks into a bucket of water. Seven of the thirty rocks were good-sized diamonds. The rest were chocolate rocks or agates. Jim and his wife were sorting through his diggings. With a bucket of water, the four found forty-plus diamonds and continued for another few hours. We left and headed for some place that has food.

We went to Blyth, walked into the restaurant and ordered food. Donna said, "Please hurry, I'm starving."

The waitress said, "We will do our best, ma'am." The waitress brought some appetizers. We all got something to eat and then our food came. We munched down on our food. Robert ordered food for four people. The waitress counted five. "This food is to go." We got a room for the night. Rob refrigerated it.

The morning came, and we headed back to our diamond mine with some food for Jim's family. Jack said, "Stop. Something doesn't feel right." Rob stopped, got his nine mm, and gave it to Jack. He got his forty-five. We walked over the rise and close to the Townson family. No one looked up. Rob walked down with Jack beside him. We got down close enough to see what was wrong. Some illegal immigrants were holding the Townsons hostage.

Jack yelled. The hostage takers turned. Six shots were fired. Six bodies fell. Another five ran. Jack shot four more. He ran out of bullets. Robert picked up a rifle from the illegals and shot the last one at sixty yards. Jack went up and brought their two vehicles down to the dig area. Border patrol heard the shots and arrived in twenty minutes at high speed.

The border patrol looked at all the bodies. Neither one of the CBP agents said a word. Jim, Jack, and Rob help load the bodies into the back of the CBP truck.

Robert said, "Here is some food for your family."

"Thank you, Robert and Jack." An hour later, we saw a fire several miles from us. Jim picked up all the drug mules, weapons, and ammo and loaded up their truck. Jim said, "We have almost forty pounds of diamonds. I am putting our property up for sale at two million dollars. We want out of this area."

Jack said, "Double your sell price, Jim. It will be worth it. Those weapons are all stolen. Give them to CBP or ATF." We went through the rocks and in the hole. We only found twenty small diamonds. Robert sold his property for three million dollars. The Townson family got three million five hundred thousand dollars.

CAROL AND MOLLY

Carol Hawly and Molly Fernley were best friends from high school. Both women were married and then divorced. Their exes were jerks and playboys. The two women were living together with the children. Carol had a girl, Billie. Molly had three children. The twins were Karen and Darin. The youngest was Robert. He was one year older than Billie.

In 1997, Billie went into the first grade, and Bobby started the second grade. Billie was in the first grade for two hours, then was moved to the second grade. Carol was nineteen, and Molly was twenty-one. She would buy the alcohol for them. The twins were in the third grade. Their class grades were very high.

Five years passed, and Karen and Darin started high school. They were two very happy children. Both children worked during the summer at Home Depot. After two years of saving money, their bank account reached eighteen thousand dollars. Graduation time—both graduated with a GPA of 3.87.

In 2003, Darin said, "Mom, we want a car. We saw one we like at the car lot in town." Lexington, Nebraska, wasn't a big town, but there was plenty to do during the summer.

Molly asked, "How does it run? What is the year of the car?"

Karen said, "We don't know, Mom. Take us down there and ride with us. We have had our driver's license for two years. We want our own car now."

"What about college? Save your money for that."

"Mom, we need transportation first. We have eighteen thousand dollars saved, and we can get another nine thousand this summer."

Darin said, "I can work while Karen starts her first year of school."

"Why don't you two take junior college classes for two years then start full time at a college?"

Robert said, "I can work and help them for school funds."

"Bobby, you are too young to work."

"Mom, I was born Robert not Bobby. Please call me what you named me." Everyone was laughing except Robert.

"Okay, son…Bobby."

Robert and Billie went to work wherever they could to help Karen and Darin start college. Three weeks after graduating, Molly received a call from the university in Kearney, Nebraska, just thirty-two miles away. Karen and Darin received a two-year academic scholarship. The twins were thrilled. Just what they needed.

Molly and Carol went to the dealer to look for a car with the children. Several cars were test driven. All of them were not worth the price the dealer was asking.

Carol said, "Let's pick one and give them your car. We know it runs. We still have my car to get around in." Molly agreed. Karen and Darin went to Kearney and registered for college, came home, and went to work for Home Depot until school started. Billie and Robert also worked to help the twins with funds when their two years were over. Carol and Molly had some lovers, but were not happy with either one.

The summer funds were growing for the twins. Billie and Robert didn't make much, but every penny helped. Robert and Billie started their third year of high school, and the twins started their second year of college. Robert and Billie went to work for Lowes in Lexington. Karen and Darin were home for a week then back to Kearny. The two had jobs with Home Depot. Two years done. Now the two will have to work extra to get through the last two years.

The money saved would get the twins through their third year. Molly and Carol did not like Nebraska. Molly drove herself and Carol to Utah. They were there for two weeks, looking for a house to rent. There were not many good houses available. The two went to the liquor store and purchased a bottle of bourbon. Carol turned to leave and ran into a young man.

She smiled and said, "Sorry for running you over."

"The pleasure is mine. Are you in a hurry?"

"Not really. Molly, are you ready?"

"Before you leave, my name is David. This is my brother, Steve." The four left the store together. Steve said, "We are teachers. We teach at Layton high school. Where are you from? Where are you staying?"

"I am Molly."

"I am Carol. We do not like Nebraska. The winters are terrible. Wet, heavy snow. Our roof cracked last year."

Steve said, "We have snow here also, but it is lighter snow. We have stronger roofs here." Molly spent the night with Steve. David took Carol home. Three nights together, and the two couples were very happy.

Molly said, "We have to go home now. Our children are wondering what happened to us."

Steve said, "I love you Molly, honey. Can I talk you into moving in with me? I need your company."

"Carol, baby, I have a big, lonely house waiting for someone like you. Are you interested?" Steve and David followed them to Nebraska. Three days packing up everything into their pickups. David rented a trailer. Molly drove to Kearny and talked to the twins. "You can finish your last two years in Utah. We found a nice house with a man in it."

"Mom, are you sure? Is he going to leave like our dad left you with nothing?"

"Life is sometimes cruel, honey. Carol and I want out of this state. We do not have money to repair the roof. He is a nice man. A high school teacher. Please come with us. I need your support." Karen and Darin said, "Okay. We will go too. We don't like this state either." An hour of packing and then they were headed back to Lexington. Everyone was waiting for Molly and the twins.

Molly introduced Steve to Karen and Darin. Darin walked up to him, looked into his eyes, and stared for a few seconds. "It is nice to meet you."

Carol said, "Are we ready to get on the road?" Everyone got into a car and headed for Utah.

On the way, Steve asked Molly, "I thought he was going to hit me. What is he angry about?"

"Their father walked out one night while I was working. Karen and Darin became protectors of Robert until he started school."

"I hope he gets over the hate in his body."

"Both of them will have to find a job. Just two more years of college then start teaching somewhere."

"I will talk to them once we get moved in. We are not far from Weber State University." Everyone switched drivers. Robert drove for several hours. Billie is only fifteen, but she drove with Robert. Ogden looked good when we entered the city.

Darin asked, "Mr. Steve, where are our rooms?"

"Sorry, but you two will be closer to the college. Don't unpack your things here. We will go up there in a few minutes." Steve's parents came over. "Mom, Dad, a surprise to see you. Molly, my mom, Karen, and my dad, Steve Senior. This is Molly, her children, Karen, Darin, and Robert."

"Nice to meet all of you. David, who captured your heart?"

"This is Carol, and her daughter, Billie. One more year of high school, then on to college."

"Bring them up after you all get moved in. Supper will be ready in a couple of hours," Karen said. Molly and Robert got moved in with Steve's help. He put Molly and Robert in his car. "Darin, follow me to your new home. It is not far from the college." The house was in the shadow valley area. A single-story three-bedroom house.

"Dave and I bought this house while we were still in college. We decided to keep it for a summer retreat. We don't get up here much anymore." The four had Karen and Darin moved in very quickly.

"Now down to my parents' home. It is just around the corner." A three-minute drive.

Karen said, "Oh my gosh, theirs is a mansion."

"Dad bought it when prices were still low. He paid cash for it."

Molly said, "I feel out of place walking into their house. Kids, clean your shoes."

Steve said, "That won't be necessary. It is a hardwood floor." We went up the back way to the back door.

Mrs. Thomas said, "Wipe your feet." We looked at Steve Junior and snickered. Darin left his shoes outside. He had mud on them. Carol, David, and Billie were already there. Molly was admiring the kitchen. She almost started to cry.

"Your kitchen is a woman's dream. It is so beautiful."

"Steve built the island two years ago after all the kids were out on their own." Stacey and Danese showed up with their children. Stacey has three girls. Her husband, Mark Young, is a finance officer as is Stacey. Danese is a teacher along with her husband, Jim Franks. Their two children are in school also. One boy and a younger sister. Dinner was served. The children ate in the living room watching cartoons on the TV. Mark turned off the TV. "Eat first, children."

Robert stood up. "Don't be a bully, Mr. Young." Robert turned on the cartoons again. Steve Senior smiled and looked at Mark. "Let it be." The day came to an end, and the children were bedded down on the deck out of the summer wind. Billie and Robert curled up next to each other.

Steve Junior looked at Molly and Carol. "What is that?"

Molly said, "Those two have been in love with each other since the third grade."

Carol said, "The two want to get married after high school. Do you want another drink, honey?" Karen and Darin went to their house and went to bed. Steve, Molly, Dave, and Carol got their two children and went home. Robert and Billie went walking the next day. Both of them were looking for a job.

Robert said, "Mom, there isn't any work here for us. How can we help Karen and Darin through college?"

Steve said, "I am paying their way through their last years. What money you make is yours." He handed Robert the keys to his car. "Drive carefully. There is a Home Depot and Lowes in Ogden." Robert and Billie filled out a job application at both stores. Home Depot called them. Rob and Billie were working the next day. Steve Davis Senior and his wife, Karen, pulled Molly and Carol away from their two sons for a few days. Dave proposed to Carol and Steve Junior made a proposal to Molly. The double wedding was set for July 30, 2003.

DAVID TEAL

May 1966, Dave just put his wife in the cemetery. He and his late wife had just celebrated their twenty-third birthday. She had a bad allergy. She was allergic to several things. The one that killed her was in a glass of wine. David was in a deep depression for several days. His brother and parents did their best to bring him out and start all over again.

David slowed down on his drinking and went back to work. After three weeks of working, he packed up his prized possessions in his truck and left town. He told no one that he was leaving. Just gone after his last day of work for the week. He received his paycheck, cashed it, and left California. He had no idea where he would go, but he just had to go. He went through Nevada, Utah, and into Wyoming. He rested for the night in a motel in Green River.

Morning came, and he went north into Idaho. After traveling to Lewiston, he spent another night there. He checked his finances. All he had was two hundred sixty-one dollars. He went back to Boise; he looked for a job. Aa a diesel mechanic, he quickly had a job working at a truck stop. He stayed there for fourteen months. He saved every penny he could.

It was summertime again. He picked up and cashed his check and hit the road again. Dave had twelve hundred dollars now. Plenty of traveling money. Back home in San Diego, California, his family was frantically searching for him. Dave was doing his best to hid from everything of his past. His late wife never gave him any children, so there was no reason to stay.

He arrived in Detroit and went to the diesel shops looking for work. He found work at Cummins Diesel company. After working there for three months, he got a pay raise. Dave was moved to engine repair supervisor. Eighteen dollars an hour was a great raise for him. His last job was only twelve dollars per hour. Dave liked the hourly pay, so he had no reason to leave.

After three years working there, he got a week off. In 1970, he took a fishing trip in Lake Michigan. Fourteen people on the boat, but only eleven were fishing. Dave caught a big fish, reeled it in, and tagged it. That is his. The fishing continued for several hours. A scream was heard. A person fell overboard. Everyone looked, but no one moved for a few seconds.

Dave Teal dropped his fishing pole and made a jump to help the person in the water. The boat had stopped, and a life ring was thrown out in the water, but it was sixty feet short. He grabbed the life ring and swam to the person in the water. A young woman was fishing and dropped her pole and reached for it but fell overboard. Dave reached for her and pulled her to him. She was almost choking him. He managed to get her to hold on to the life ring. The boat crew pulled both of them back to the boat.

Shelly was so happy for Dave for saving her life. After getting back on board, the crew gave them some dry clothes inside the cabin. There the two stayed until the boat was back in port. Dave and Shelly picked up their wet clothes and left the boat with his fish. Shelly asked him to come home with her. He was off for two more days, so he said okay. Shelly put their clothes in the washer and went into the kitchen and cooked up the fish. She fixed a salad, while Dave set the table. Their supper was great.

Shelly laughed. "I lost their fishing pole. I had a bite but didn't get to reel it in."

Dave laughed. "It was a minnow." Both of them laughed. Supper was ready, so the two set down and ate fish and salad.

Shelly said, "Stay the night with me please. I am lonely. I need your company." She got tears in her eyes.

Dave held her. "I will stay as long as you want me to. I love you honey. I need to tell you, I lost my wife from an allergy. She was my life. Gone in a heartbeat. I have been on the road ever since. You just stopped my roaming around. I don't want to keep moving now."

Shelly said, "I love you too, sweetie. Thank you for saving my life. I owe you so much that I don't think I will ever be able to repay you."

Dave held her and said, "You just ended my loneliness. I have been paid in full." The two kissed several times and went to the bedroom. The next morning, their two lives started over again. The past of both of them had just been erased and a new life for the young couple had started. Shelly was twenty-three and pregnant. Dave was twenty-five and very happy.

Both went back to work on Monday.

His boss said, "A good weekend, Dave?"

"It was great. I went on a fishing trip. I caught a fish and a woman. The fish we ate and the woman—well, that's private." His boss and coworkers laughed. Back to work for everyone. A break for lunch. He was asked about his woman. Dave talked about his first wife and her short life. He was roaming, and now he wanted to stay with Shelly for life. The crew never asked nothing else about his past.

Dave continued working there another two months, then he said, "I want to take some time off. I need a rest. We are getting married in five days, and you all are invited to our wedding." The whole crew applauded.

"When and where?" Sam asked. Dave gave them the date and place. "Bring your spouse and children also. I need a flower girl and ringbearer. Her family and mine are two thousand miles away."

His boss got ahold of Shelly and told her, "We are holding David captive until the wedding day." She laughed.

"Don't hurt him please. I am three months pregnant."

"We will be there. How much do you need for a wedding dress? My wife will be over to your house this evening. Bonnie will go with you to find a wedding dress. Your budget is two thousand dollars." She started crying. Dave and Shelly only saved enough to buy the rings. Their bank account was empty. Just waiting for payday.

Bonnie arrived at Shelly's house and talked to Shelly. The two went looking for a wedding dress. Shelly said, "We cannot afford anything for a fancy dress. I have a nice one at home. We can't pay you back, so please stop looking for something I can't afford."

Bonnie said, "The amount has been set already. Please, Shelly, you cannot go to a wedding in an old dress. You will not have to pay us back. The whole shop has put in some money for a beautiful dress for you." Shelly started crying. The search for her dress continued. The next day, she had five wives with her to find a dress. Dave has a rental suit. She hadn't seen Dave for three days now. She found a dress that was in their budget. Eleven hundred dollars. Shelly looked for the cheapest but a beautiful wedding dress.

On July 6, 1970, Dave was at the church waiting. Shelly had six women helping her get ready. She was a nervous wreck. Shelly Drake was never married. This is her first time. The flower girl and ringbearer were chosen from all the children.

Dave's boss, Mike, took her last name and searched the state of California. He found Shelly's parents. That was her big surprise. Shelly was ready to walk up to the altar, her mother and father showed up. She started crying again and held both of them.

Her father, Jon, said, "Are you ready to go for a walk?" She couldn't answer. She walked up to the altar with her father. Her eyes were wet with tears.

The priest asked, "Do you give your daughter to this man?"

"I don't know him, but our daughter loves him so. Yes, I do." A little laughter. The ceremony was done in ten minutes, and everyone went to the reception across the street. A driver was already selected. A high school senior from one of the shop worker's children. Dave and Shelly were ready to get home, so their driver took them home. Her parents were put up in a motel for a week.

When Dave and Shelly went back to work, Dave got to meet her parents and siblings. Her parents were so happy to see their daughter; the two cried through most of the ceremony. Now everyone was happy.

Her dad said, "Please, you two come back to California, honey."

Dave said, "I like it here. This is the best job I have ever had, and I don't want to give it up. This is the best pay I have ever had. Almost twice as any other job I had."

Jon said, "You two come visit and bring our grandchild, please."

"We will, Dad, Mom…next summer?" She looked at Dave.

He said, "We will be there, maybe." Then he laughed. Her parents headed for home to California.

Dave called his parents. "I found a wonderful woman. I am married again. She is a very good cook. Now I don't have to eat burnt food any more. We will be there next summer. I love you, Mom and Dad." Back to work on Monday and doing great. Dave and Shelly were happy with each other.

On January 11, 1971, Dave rushed Shelly to the hospital. Thirty minutes had passed, and their little son popped his head out. 11:41 a.m. He was six pounds four ounces, seventeen inches. He has a very loud voice. Dave took some pictures and had copies made. He mailed copies to both families with notes in a letter.

Shelly took a break from work for a while. Our baby son was keeping Mom busy. When Dave got home, he did some of the duties. He was learning to change a diaper without getting choked up. He was very happy. Summer was now here, and their son David Junior could crawl at a high speed. Dave and Shelly took a summer break from work. Ten days off for their trip to San Diego to visit their families.

Their flight was fast, and their parents of both families were waiting for them. The mothers were excited to see their first grandchild. Up at Dave's parents' home, we had a room to spend our time in at night. Neither Shelly or Dave knew our parents were living just two houses apart. Shelly said, "Where have you been all my life, honey?" then she laughed. We went through school together. Just two grades apart for all twelve years of school.

Dave said, "I was looking for a rose. I passed up the Orchid, because that is what you are." Shelly gave him a kiss. "Thank you, baby." The warm weather pulled us to the beach. Six hours and some swimming in the ocean. After we got back home, Shelly's dad set up for a BBQ in his backyard. Our vacation was coming to an end. We packed up our bags and got a ride to the airport. We said our good byes and flew back home to Detroit. We had a sitter, so both of us could work.

Shelly said, "Honey, I am ready for another baby."

ETHEL AND EDWARD

Eddy was just three years old. His parents were not very rich. He received one gift for Christmas. No other children in the family. His parents, Ed Senior and Ethel, were working at Walmart receiving minimum wage. The two received employee discount for the gift for their son. The couple graduated from high school and were married one week later. Ethel was pregnant before graduation. Their baby was born on November 6, 1955.

With a baby to take care of, Ethel has to work shorter hours. She was unhappy, but she endured. Eddy Senior is working two jobs to make up what his wife couldn't do. Their marriage was falling apart. Ed Senior got very upset and walked out, leaving Ethel with a baby and a very low income. Three months had passed. Ethel asked for welfare assistance. She did manage to get food stamps and welfare assistance. Her husband was out of state. Nobody knew where he was. He just ran away. Ethel and her son were just surviving. The food stamps helped keep them alive. She thought about putting Eddy Junior up for adoption but changed her mind. Her son was her whole life, and she didn't want to give that up.

Ethel talked to her parents, Thomas and Marji. She was able to move back home with her son. Ethel had to get a degree or a tech school. She started taking classes to complete her first two years. She wants to be a teacher. She was very intelligent, so her classes were not very hard for her.

Her father said, "We will help you, but you will have to pay us back. We are spending our retirement funds to get you through college."

"Thank you, Dad, Mom. I will pay back every penny." Ethel was also working during the summer time. Her money went to her mom for food and personal feminine things Ethel needed. Ethel filed for a divorce before her second year of school started. Her first year grades were 3.52. She was hoping for higher grades for her second year. The fall semester is going good for her. All the instructors were thrilled for her and her high grades.

On November 11, 1960, she got home after the classes were done for the day. Her parents had two things for her. Her dad handed her the divorce papers. The divorce was approved. She was really excited. After dinner, her son ran to his room and came back with a small gift for his mom. "Happy birthday, Mama." Marji brought a birthday cake from the refrigerator with twenty-two candles on it. Ethel cried and hugged her son and parents. Everyone had a piece of cake with some ice cream.

Ethel is the oldest student in all her classes and has the highest grades. Her grades for the fall semester was 3.61. Christmastime here and a few days to relax before the spring semester started. Ethel bought a gift for each of her parents and two gifts for her son, Eddy. She received a gift from her parents. Everyone was happy.

The spring semester started, and Ethel was back in school. This semester went by very fast for her. Her second year ended with her grades, averaging 3.62. Summertime and back to work for Ethel. She was now working at Home Depot. Higher pay and easier work. She made six thousand dollars during the summer. She and her parents were thrilled for the money.

In 1961, her third year started, and the class work was a little harder, so she studied harder. Eddy was now in the first grade. Neither of her parents went to college. Both of them took tech schools. Halfway through the fall semester, Ethel was asked to teach the third grade at the local elementary school.

She asked the dean, "Am I ready for this, sir?"

"We will see, young lady. Your grades say you are ready." She was driven to the school. She was taken to the classroom.

The principal said, "Take a deep breath and speak with confidence. You are the teacher, Ethel." She went into the classroom. The students calmed down and listened to Ethel, Mrs. Meek. She wrote her name under the original teacher's name.

"I am Mrs. Meek. I will be here until Miss James can return. What book are you working on?" She started with the math book. The books were all marked for the substitute teacher. Ethel looked through the first page then talked to the students. She showed them how to add and subtract. She had some homework for them. Reading was next. She opened the book, then picked a student to read a paragraph. Another recess.

The students went to the gym to play. The snow on the ground with cold temperatures kept everyone inside. Ethel sat down and gave a sigh of relief. Then she jumped up and went to the gym to watch over her students. She went to play with them. It was a lot of fun for her and the class. Back to the classroom, they opened the coloring books.

She asked the students, "Would you draw a picture of their favorite pet? If you do not have one, make one up." All the students went to drawing something. Ethel walked around the room, looking at their pictures, saying, "That is a good picture, thank you." Those things helped her get through five weeks of teaching. She was happy for the opportunity to teach, but now, she was behind on her college classes.

Thanksgiving was here. She enjoyed the four-day weekend.

Back in the college class, Ethel asked, "How much did I miss? How will I make it up? I don't want to take this semester over." She was given some tests and finished the semester with an average of 3.60. She really had to study harder than ever before. One more semester, then the final year. Excitement was running through her body. The spring semester started, and she worked hard to keep her grades up. Her third year finished, and she did good on her grades. It was summertime, and Ethel went to work at Home Depot for three months.

Her summer work brought home another six thousand dollars. She bought her needs and some new clothes for her growing son. He will be in the second grade in September. Ethel went to school and purchased her books and registered for her last fall semester. Classes started, and she made it to every class. She had lots of homework.

Ethel had to write a thesis for her English class. She had three months to complete it.

When she started college, one foreign language was required to graduate. Her parents' neighbor speaks four languages. Their son started college the same year as Ethel. She knew him from years before. She asked Pierre to teach her a foreign language.

"What is the easiest language to learn?"

He said, "French or Spanish. I think Spanish will be easier for you. It is more like English." Now the two were in their last year, Ethel learned Spanish and some of French. Thanksgiving was three days away, and she turned in her thesis about the civil war. Fifteen pages of writing. Her hand hurt when she finally finished it. Pierre turned in his thesis three days earlier.

The semester came to an end, and Ethel was surprised of her English grade of 3.81. Her other classes combined were 3.72 average. One more semester. The spring semester. Ethel relaxed during the holidays. She bought a gift for Eddy. She apologized to her parents for not getting them a gift.

Her father, Thomas, said, "Your graduation from college will be your gift to us." She held her dad and cried.

"Just one more semester, Dad, Mom. Just one more."

On New Year's Eve, Pierre asked her, "Would you like to go to a dance with me? I don't drink alcohol." She said okay. There was a ballroom for those interested in dancing the night away. He had a car, so no one had to walk. Four hours of talking and dancing, then she kissed him when the countdown to ring in the new year was done.

He smiled and said, "Thank you, young lady. Nobody has ever kissed me before." She kissed him again. This kiss was a long kiss.

She asked him, "Have you ever had sex? Would you like to? I need some." Three hours in a motel room, then the two went home.

She said, "Honey, you are good. I am happy again."

School started, and they were back for their last semester. No fooling around. Just studying together. Their grades were high for both of them. Ethel finished the year and graduated with a 3.76. For the four years, her average was 3.66. She was very happy. Pierre finished with 3.72 for the four years. In June 1963, her parents and son attended Ethel's graduation. Mom and Dad took several pictures. Pierre took a group picture for them. Ethel did the same for him and his family.

She put her resume out. The elementary school called her before she got home. There was a message on the recorder. Marji played the message. "Ethel, listen to this. Are you ready to start teaching?" Mom played the message again.

She got tears in her eyes and said, "Yes!"

"I will drive you down to the school." Marji drove her to the school. Ethel went in and talked to the principal. "The fifth-grade teacher is moving. The position is yours if you want it."

"I will think about it. Yes, I will take it." A two-second delay.

"We follow the college students from year to year. The third grade loved the way you got out and played with them. Your grades are super. We will see you the last week of August. Okay?"

"Thank you very much. I will be here on time."

"You must be proud of your daughter, ma'am."

Marji said, "Yes, I am, and her father is also proud of her." Eddy would start the third grade in September. Ethel worked at Home Depot for two months. She bought some clothes for the start of her teaching career, if she could make it through this first year. Ethel took Eddy to a movie again this summer. She took him to his second movie for this summer vacation.

Eddy also got some new clothes. He was growing about two inches each summer. He is four feet three inches. The tallest person in his class. Ethel showed up on time. The staff and teachers had their meeting at this time before each year starts. Ethel was the only new teacher this year.

"Mrs. Ethel Meek is our new teacher. Guess what, Ethel, you get to teach your third-grade class students again. As fifth graders now, the class will be happy to see you again." School started for Ethel's first year teaching.

She walked into the fifth-grade classroom. The whole class cheered. She raised her hands for quiet. "I am Mrs. Meek. I will be here all year—if I don't beat up one of you." The class broke out in laughter.

"This is my first year as a full-time teacher. How was your summer? Did anything exciting happen to anyone?" Several hands went up. She pointed to one at a time.

"Okay, class, I think I will start with history. Open your history book to the first chapter." There was no homework the first week. The first half of the school year went well for Ethel. The holiday season was here. Her son, Eddy, received several gifts. Her parents gave Ethel and Eddy a gift each. Ethel gave her parents a gift each also and her first payment for her college school loan.

Ethel finished her first year teaching. Eddy finished the third grade. Ethel went looking for a car with the help of her parents. The family spent two weeks looking but found nothing anybody liked.

Dad said, "I would like to look at an older car. Something in the fifties. Those cars are built stronger and get better milage." After several days of looking and test-driving them, a '56 Ford was selected for Ethel.

The elementary school was a mile from home. Tom took the car to his auto mechanic friend, Dave. Six weeks had passed when he drove the car to Tom's house.

The repairs were extensive, but he took the car to the automotive tech school. Ethel only paid for the parts. Complete overhaul of the brake system and a total engine rebuild and new transmission. The cost was $654. In 1964, the car was licensed and insured. She had a good car to get herself and Eddy to school every day come September.

Eddy started the fourth grade, and his mom started her second year teaching. Ethel just completed her seventh year teaching. Her debt to her parents was paid four years earlier. Her savings was to put aside to get her son, Edward, through college.

In 1971, Ed was in his third year of high school. His first two years' grades were 3.92. He was supersmart. The third year went well for him. He had a girlfriend. Her name was August. She was competing with him for top grades and as valedictorian. To this point, their grades were only .002 apart. Eddy was in second place. Their third year ended with top grades for both of them. The junior senior prom was the last week of May. The two spent the whole night dancing. He and August were taking pregnancy precautions.

After the prom, he drove her home. A few kisses then she went into her house and met her parents. "Hi, Mom, Dad, my feet hurt." She sat down. "We danced every dance the whole night. No, Mom, we did not have any sex. It is the wrong time of the month."

"Thank you, honey. See you in the morning," her mom said. One more week and then it was summertime before the last year of high school. Their summer was very good. The parents of both families went to Yellow Stone National Park. Two rented trailers and a camping spot next to each other. A week there and a ton of fun for everyone. Just a few miles away, the next camping area has plenty of fishing and swimming. Ed and August went up the creek and went swimming and did other things in the nude. August's mother, Delores, saw them in the water but didn't say anything then. She would talk to her later.

Ed's mom asked, "How was the swimming, son?"

"Great, Mom. The water was a little cooler than we are used to, so we held on to each other."

"With or without clothes?"

August said, "How long have you been watching us? We want to get married after school. We love each other." Nothing else was said.

Now back home, Ed and August went to work at Lowes for the remainder of summer. Together their money totaled five thousand dollars. Very excited with their money, some of it was spent on new clothes for their last year of high school. Love was keeping them together.

Their last year started, and they were two excited kids. Ed said, "Who will get the valedictorian?"

"Can we split it? I just want to graduate, and then we can get married," August said.

"What do you think about college? We have no good job without college. I want a good job so I can support us."

"I want a good job also. I love you very much, honey."

"How much?" He held his hands a few inches apart.

She put her hands as far apart as she could. "That much."

Ed put his hands out to pass her hands. "I love you this much more." He was six feet, one inch. August was only five feet, eight inches.

"Your arms are longer than mine." She wrapped her arms around him. He did the same by putting his arms around her. A few kisses and then both were getting ready for their last year. The school year started, and the whole class was very happy for the end of high school. The whole senior class took the SAT just before their final class tests. Now they would just wait and hope a college will call some of them.

Graduation time was here, and all students would graduate. No one was left behind. The final grades were out. August and Edward were hoping that either one would be the top student. The principal purposely left their names off the final test results. Both of them were shocked. "Where are our names?" August said.

The principal called everyone to the gym. "We have a dilemma to deal with. I know one couple wanted to be our top student. We have five class students for valedictorian. Their four year grades are 3.935 to 3.936. I have no idea on how to resolve this. I am asking the students to decide who should be the top student."

A student from the sophomore class said, "Let those students decide. Draw straws or all of them talk at their graduation."

"What are your grades like?" someone said.

"My grades? This is only my second year. I am holding a 3.98." The five students picked the two top students, August and Fred. The others were angry but let it be. When graduation ceremonies started, all five went up to talk. Three minutes each. The students got together and split the speech into five parts. All five went up to give their part of the speech. The parents of the students were surprised when the group walked up and made their three-minute talk and then walked off the podium.

The walk for their graduation was a delight for all the students. Finally, they were done with high school. Of the sixty-eight students, sixty-two went to college. Those top five students got a four-year scholarship in different colleges. Edward and August managed to get the same college. The two were married the summer before their college years started.

FOR JOHN MARSHALL

Jeffery Marshall was the youngest son of John Marshall. He was born in May 1948. He finished high school with top honors. Jeff went on to college. Jeff had to drop out after two and a half years completed. His mother, Sarah, had passed away, and Jeff had to take care of his little sister, Amber. Jeff started working for Home Depot as a manager. His business management education in college helped him land a good job. Jeff was twenty, and Amber was thirteen.

The oldest boy, Carl, was no help. He did not finish high school. He got hooked on drugs and was a total mess. Amber was in the eighth grade. Their mother died from loneliness. Sarah missed the company of her husband, John Marshall. He was an army specialist and disappeared in the jungle of Vietnam in 1963. Five years had passed since he disappeared.

Jeff heard rumors that his older brother wanted to sell Amber for money so he could buy more drugs. When he heard that, he went to Carl and confronted him with this news. "Don't even try to sell her. If you do, I will kill you and the buyer."

Carl just laughed and said, "It is too late. The deal is already done." Jeff hurried home and found two men trying to take Amber out of the house. She was putting up a good fight. Jeffery interrupted them with several hits to the face of one and a swift kick to the groin of the other.

He continued beating them until both of them were unconscious, then he called the police. He told the police what had happened and accused his older brother, Carl Marshall, for selling his little sister for drugs. The police had to call for medical personnel to treat the injured men and check out Amber. The police took the two men to jail and talked to Carl. He denied everything, but he was taken to jail, because the police found a lot of drugs in his house. Carl was already high from some of the drugs.

After Amber was through shaking, she asked Jeff, "Where did you learn to fight like that?"

"Two men taught me while I was still a young boy."

"Did you know them?"

"No, the men said, your dad asked us to teach you how to protect yourself." Amber started crying. Jeff held her. He cried also.

"Is our father still alive?" she asked.

"I don't know. Sis, it has been six years."

"Why did Carl sell me? I didn't do anything to him."

"He wanted more drugs. He can think about his mistake in prison for several years."

Amber said. "Good, we don't need him here. He never did anything to help us."

"I will pick you up after school, and you can stay with me until I get off work. I do not know who bought you. He still wants to get you. I will talk to the principal tomorrow morning. I don't want you to listen to anyone, man or woman, that comes to school saying that I have been injured and you need to go to the hospital."

"What should I do if someone comes?"

"Fight back, and go to the principal's office, then call me."

"I'm scared, Jeff, I don't know if I can fight back."

Six months had passed with no abduction attempts on Amber. School was out for the summer, Amber went to work with Jeff every day. She started working at Home Depot. Amber could only work a few hours each day, but she liked the money. After her hours were up, she would go into Jeff's office and wait for him. She would go home with her brother. Jeff had got a conceal carry permit because nobody knew who paid for Amber. Jeff had a security system put throughout his house, with several cameras. He was able to look at them through his TV at work.

School was now back in session, and Jeff was still taking Amber to school and picking her up after school. Mid October, someone ran into Jeff's car on the way to school. He started to get out when a man from the other car came out with a gun in hand. Jeff told Amber to get down and lock your door. Jeff had his gun in his hand but out of sight. The man came up on Amber's side of the car. Jeff watched him. He got to the door, pointed his gun at Jeff, then Jeff aimed his gun at him and fired two shots, killing him.

A few minutes later, the police were there. The police checked the dead man's fingerprints. "Wow, he is—was—a paid assassin."

His partner said, "Not anymore." Then he laughed.

Jeff said, "I didn't want to kill him. I want to know who paid for my sister." He paused. "Can I talk to Carl?" Maybe he can tell me. He received all those drugs as payment." A few days later, Jeff was granted permission to see his brother in the Nevada state prison.

Jeff asked, "Why did you sell my sister?"

"For the drugs."

"Look what it got you. Who paid you?"

"I can't tell you. If I do, he will kill me."

"That won't bother me one bit. Who is it, Carl?"

"Go home and protect your sister. You already know. You beat the crap out of him with a kick to the balls."

Jeff smiled and left. Two weeks later, Carl was dead. The man who had Carl killed was stabbed too. He later died in the hospital. It wasn't over yet, because another man tried to abduct Amber. She was at home alone, when a man broke into the house. He grabbed Amber from behind, but he picked the wrong time. She was making a salad cutting the vegetables with a knife. She brought the knife over her left shoulder and stabbed him in the neck. He fell on the floor, holding his neck, trying to stop the bleeding. "Who are you?"

"I paid for you, so you are mine."

Amber said, "Here I am. Come and get me." She was shaking while waving the knife at him. She called the police and said, "There is a man bleeding on my kitchen floor. No, take your time." Then she laughed. "Hurry, he is making a mess."

"Where is he bleeding from?"

"I stabbed him in the neck. He tried to abduct me."

The police and paramedics arrived at the same time.

As the medics were tending to him, he said, "I bought her. She belongs to me. She is mine. She is mine." He died on the way to the hospital. Amber called her brother and told him what happened.

"Are you all right, honey?"

She said, "Yes, but I have to clean the kitchen floor."

"I will be home in a few minutes." He almost got a speeding ticket. He told the officer why he was going so fast.

The officer said, "Keep the speed down."

Jeff arrived home and helped Amber clean the blood off the floor. He said, "Carl lied to me. He told me the buyer was one of the men I beat up."

Amber said, "He won't bother us anymore. He died on the way to the hospital."

"Are you sure he is dead?"

"I hope he is. Can we go to the hospital and check? You got me worried now." Jeff drove to the hospital and checked the morgue. Both of them got a look at his face. He was definitely dead.

"Jeffery, will you teach me to drive? If there are any more of them out there, I want to run him over." Then both of them started laughing and crying at the same time. "No more shooting through my window. You made me pee in my pants."

Jeff laughed and said, "I'm sorry, sis, it won't happen again. I promise."

Amber went to school without much to worry about. She was still on alert for all strangers of both sexes. Jeff was still picking her up and taking her to his work. She would work a few hours before heading for home. Jeff finally got the reward for the man he shot. The man Amber stabbed was a wanted man also. She received the thirty-thousand-dollar reward. With the fifty grand Jeff got, Jeff would be able to go back to school. He went to University of Nevada, Reno.

Amber started her junior year of high school. Jeffery and Amber were always on the watch for strangers getting to close to either one of them. Jeff had a problem as the manager of the store. He was talking to strangers all the time. He was always on edge, but he greeted everyone like a friend.

In 1971, Jeff taught Amber to drive a car. She took the driving test and past it first time. "Jeff, what car is good and safe in an accident?"

"Why, do you plan on getting into an accident?" He laughed.

"I don't want to get hurt if some drunk hits me by running a red light."

"I know what you mean, sis. The army is selling some old tanks." Then he laughed. "What type of vehicle do you want? Most of them are safe."

"What do you think about the older cars? I saw a 1951 Chevrolet on a lot last week. It is still there," Amber said.

"Are you sure you want an old car? The 1970s are nice-looking vehicles."

"Yes, I know, but all the other classmates that have a car, I don't like the looks of them. I want to be different."

"You are different, you are special. You are my sister. We are the last of our family." Jeffery started crying. Amber held him and cried also. Amber bought the 1951 Chevrolet two door.

"I am going to asked for vacation time. Where do you want to go, sis?"

"I have no idea. Just get us out of Nevada for a few days."

"What do you think about going to the California coast for a week?"

She said, "That is good with me." One week in San Diego and neither one wanted to leave there. The weather was so nice and mild that Amber asked Jeff, "Another few days?"

After eleven days there, Jeff said, "I have to go back to work."

"Okay, brother, if I have to." The two laughed.

Their trip home was slow, but at home, things were back to normal.

Jeff moved to the night shift to finish college. Two years later, he received his bachelor's degree in business management. Home Depot gave him a raise. He told the upper management, "Thank you all very much. No, I am not going to quit or move. I like it here."

Amber said, "Wait until school is out. One more week and then where do you want to go?"

"I asked you first." Then he laughed. "Would you like to go to Hawaii for a week?"

Amber said, "Yes!" She held Jeff. "I love you, brother."

Jeff got time off to start after school was finished for the summer. He had tickets for their flight and hotel rooms set for each of them. Amber graduated from high school that year.

"Jeff, why two rooms?" Then she smiled. "Okay." Jeffery Marshall was twenty-three, and Amber would be eighteen on July 7, 1973.

The trip was long, but it was nice to get away from the hassle of Reno, Nevada. The flight landed at the Honolulu airport. Their ride was waiting for them. The bus took them to their hotel.

After checking in and changing clothes, both of them made a trip to the beach together. Jeffery said, "Be careful. I love you, sis. I don't want to lose you, but enjoy yourself." The water was nice but very salty. Amber asked, "Jeff, are all the oceans this salty?"

He laughed, "Yes, sis, all of them."

"I don't like all this salt on my body. I feel sticky."

A local boy heard Amber and Jeff talking. He said, "Come to my house and clean the salt off. I have a fresh water pool."

Amber said, "Go f——yourself. I don't like ugly people."

He attempted to slap her, but she blocked his swing and kicked him between the legs, which brought him to his knees. She then gave him a fast right-hand fist and broke his nose. Jim had been teaching her how to defend herself. A little karate and judo, plus kickboxing. Amber went to her room, showered, and put on clean clothes. She went back to the beach and watched Jeff try his luck on a surfboard. He had a young woman helping him learn how to surf. His white body set him out as a tourist on vacation.

Jeff said, "I thank you for your help, but I guess I will never be a good surfer." He put his rental board up.

Karen Douglas said, "This is my home now. I went to college here and decided to stay. I started my own business, and I'm doing pretty good. How old is your sister?"

"Amber is seventeen. This is our second trip out of Nevada. Our first trip, we spent eleven days on the beach in California. I own two casinos." Amber glared at him. "Do you want to hear another lie?" Then he laughed. "I am a manager at Home Depot in Reno, Nevada."

Amber said, "That is the truth. I am Amber. What is your name?"

"I am Karen. Nice to meet you. You hit the wrong person. He is a gang member."

"Should I worry? How many members?"

Karen said, "Just fifteen. I would not worry. All of them are good men. They are all in a karate club. Most of them are at least a black belt."

Amber said, "Oh, shit, I guess I really screwed up."

Karen said, "Don't worry, Amber, I will talk to them. Their club is my business venture. Do you want to meet them?"

Jeff said, "Why not? I need some help teaching Amber."

"Jeff, how much do you know? I am the sensei. I am a fourth-degree black belt."

Jeff said, "Wow. Amber?"

"He won't hurt me, will he?"

"No, my little brother will hold back. He is just a second-degree black belt."

A few hours later, Jeff and Amber rode with Karen to her office. Practice time was a few minutes away. Her club was getting ready to compete against several other karate clubs.

Amber and Jeff walked into the training room.

Marc looked at them. "There she is. The one that folded me up like an accordion." Everyone started laughing. "My sister called and said you would be here shortly. It was my fault for trying to hit you from your remarks. Why did you become so aggressive?"

Jeffery said, "Our older brother was a drug addict. He sold her for a kilo of cocaine. We killed three people to protect my sister."

Amber started crying. No one said a word.

Marc said, "I am so sorry for my actions. Am I that ugly?"

"Karen, can you take us to our hotel? We need to rest for a while."

Amber wiped her eyes. "Jeff, no, I will be okay shortly. Can we stay? No, Marc, you are not ugly. That was all I could think of real quick. I am sorry for my words and actions."

The team started training for the upcoming competition. There were several weight classes. Marc was a middle weight. Amber was wowed by his ability and the things he knew. Jeff and Amber went over to their trophy case. There wasn't much room left in it. There were forty-six trophies in their case. It covered all weight classes.

The trophies had names on them. After three hours of training at different weight classes, everyone went to their dressing room and changed clothes. Karen had five women in her club. Each of them impressed Amber and Jeff.

Marc asked Amber to go out for dinner. She said yes as she looked at Jeff. Karen said, "Your brother and I will be with you."

Jeff asked, "Where are we going?"

Marc said, "To get something to eat." They all laughed. "To the Tiki Village." Dinner was supreme. They stuffed themselves. After eating, they went to their house and met their parents.

Her mom said, "After Karen graduated and started her business, she asked her family to move to Hawaii. She said that she will support the family. She did just that." There were always new students coming in each year. Her club was well-known as one of the best on Oahu. Her mother asked, "Are these two new guinea pigs?" Then she laughed.

"Mom, no. These people are here on vacation. Be nice."

"I am just kidding."

Jeffery and Amber both got some lovemaking that night.

After going back to the hotel the next day, Amber asked Jeff, "I would like to stay there with Marc. I like him very much. I feel safe with him. Please, Jeff."

"I can't protect you if you are three thousand miles away. I know you are ready for college, but are you ready to get married?" A short break. "Marc is three years your senior, and he has one more year of college to finish. What is going to be your major?"

"A stay-at-home mother." She laughed. "I don't know, Jeff. I love you, but I would like to try life on my own. He asked me to stay with him." She was crying. "Can I stay here, Jeff? Please."

He held her. "I love you too. You have to promise to keep me informed on your feelings, like are you happy, is he abusing you? If you want to leave, you will always have a room in our house. Okay?"

"Yes, Jeff. I will call each month about my feelings and my relations with Marc. I promise." A few days later, Jeff left to go back to Nevada and work. Amber called to say hi. She liked Hawaii. The warm weather, a nice, good man, and the safety from bad people. She started college at University of Hawaii.

Amber felt safe here. She had fifteen men to protect her.

Jeff went to visit Hawaii every summer to spend time with his little sister and Karen. He liked Karen. She was in love with Jeff. He was afraid to asked her to marry him. He didn't want to get turned down. Every summer, Karen would hope that this year he would ask her to marry him. This summer, Jeff went to Hawaii for the fourth year. In 1977, Jeff went to his sister's graduation from the University of Hawaii.

Jeff stayed with Karen every time he went to Hawaii. He was falling for her, and she had already fallen for him. Karen was waiting for Jeffery to propose to her. That moment had not happened yet. Jeff was now twenty-nine. Karen was two months younger. Jeff said, "Thank you for letting me stay with you. I really enjoyed my time with you."

He kneeled down to simulate tying his shoelaces. Jeff put his right hand in his pocket, looked up at Karen, brought a small box out of his pocket, and opened it. Karen's eyes lit up when Jeff opened it and asked, "Karen, honey, will you marry me?"

She started crying and said, "I have been waiting for you for four years, yes."

Jeff stood up and placed the ring on her finger and held her. Karen said, "What took you so long? I love you, honey. I fell for you the first time we met."

"Fear. I was afraid you would not accept me. That is worse than being shot." The two held each other for a minute with many kisses.

Their wedding date was set for June 28, 1977. Marc had proposed to Amber earlier, but she didn't tell Jeff. She wanted to wait for Jeff and Karen to set a date. Marc and Amber wanted to make it a double wedding.

Marc and Amber set their date for June 28 and talked to the church and priest. He said, "I am thrilled you picked me. Yes, I will perform a double wedding. I know Karen and Marc very well." Two weeks later, the two couples showed up at the church with the best men and bridesmaids, plus five hundred guests and their parents. The ceremonies took almost an hour, but both couples were legally married. Two couples happy and three days in solitude from all life around them.

Jeffery transferred to Home Depot in Honolulu, Hawaii.

He was demoted to assistant manager. He didn't care. He had a job and a beautiful wife. His sister, Amber, had a degree in finance and started working for the bank of Hawaii. The two newlywed couples had dinner together. Four happy people had a nice dinner. Every one talked about their future and put Amber in charge of their finances. Two years later, their funds were over a half million.

Early March 1980, a man showed up in downtown Honolulu. He was arrested for vagrancy. No identification, just the dog tags on his neck. The tags said he was John Allen Marshall. The news was put out on all television stations. Amber called Jeffery. "Is he our father?"

"I don't know. I have some old pictures of our father."

Amber was crying. "Take me with you."

"I will. Come over here, and we can go together."

Amber showed up five minutes later, and the two went to the police station and hoped to get a look at this man. It was not their father.

Amber cried. "Where did you get my father's dog tags?"

He said, "He gave them to me a few weeks ago and said take them to Hawaii."

Jeff said, "Don't lie to us. Is he alive, or did you get them off his body?"

"He is alive. He doesn't want to be found. He would not be able to live in the civilian life. He has found and released several hundred POWs. He said he will not stop until all POWs are all free."

Jeffery and Amber started crying. "If you ever see him, tell him his family wants him back here. We love him. We will be waiting."

Two more years had passed. Jeff and Amber always waited, but John never showed up. Amber gave birth to a son and a daughter. Karen had twins. Two girls, and just last year, she gave birth to a son.

In 1986, A man showed up from another group of POWs that had escaped from Vietnam. The military checked all of them. All but one had dog tags. His fingerprints were checked. John Allen Marshall showed up on the screen.

Jeff was notified and asked to come to the military hospital. He and Amber showed up with hope in their hearts. Jeff brought some pictures, but it had been twenty-one years since he became lost in the jungles. The pictures were compared to his face. Not a real comparison, but the prints were the true identification. Jeff went in the room to talk to him. "What is your real name? What is your wife's name? What about children—did your wife have any?"

He said, "Three—Carl, Jeffery, and Amber."

"Why did you hide from everyone for so long?"

"I was afraid that I would not fit into this society."

Jeff hit him with a right cross, knocking him off his chair. "Your wife, my mother, died from loneliness from missing you. Your children are very unhappy. Go back to your f——jungle and stay out of our lives."

Amber went to him and put her arms around his neck and said, "Don't go, Father. I want you to stay here with me." She looked at Jeff. "Please?"

Jeff started crying and gave his dad a hug. "Yes, please stay. You have five grandchildren."

Jeffery found a house for him close to his home. John received some back pay for his time lost in Vietnam, for nine years.

John got a job working for the military. He was an instructor teaching SERE at the army base and naval base. Survive, evade, resist, escape. His pay was very good. He met all his grandchildren and was very happy to see them. He was sorry Sarah had passed away.

He found a nice young woman and started dating Tammy on a regular basis. It didn't take long before he asked her hand in marriage. She said yes. He talked to his children about his plans. Jeff said, What the hell are you doing? Don't you care about us?" Then he smiled. "If you love her, that is good enough for me."

Amber said, "I am happy for you, Dad. Stay out of the jungle. That war is over." John Marshall and Tammy Meek were married October 11, 1988.

GUSS STEVENSON

Roger saved five thousand dollars for his gambling fun. He wasn't addicted, just had a lot of fun. Everyone wants to win something, but if that is true, then the casinos would go broke. Roger went to Oklahoma several times from Missouri. He decided to fly to Las Vegas this time. Roger visited several casinos and won at every stop. He left with four thousand dollars above his gambling funds.

A week in Las Vegas and he decided to go to Reno. He flew a short flight there and rode a bus from the airport to downtown Reno. Roger rented a room and went to the slot machines. He sat down by this older gentleman at the quarter slots. Roger put one hundred dollars in the machine and started playing the max.

At the same time, he started talking to the man. Roger was a retired Navy vet.

Guss said, "I joined the Navy in 1948. I went to the academy and graduated." A break for a drink. "In 1952, I graduated from naval cadet school as a pilot. I made lieutenant JG. My first test was flying a fighter jet over North Korea. With guns blazing and bombs falling, I did good." The war ended, and he managed to get home for some rest and relaxation. Guss continued, "My training went on after two weeks' rest. I gave it my all, but fell short on being a top gun pilot."

Roger said, "You tried, but everyone can't be on the top. I never got off the bottom." Both men laughed.

Guss said, "I stayed in the Navy and continued my flight training. Flying a jet is a lot of fun for me."

Roger said, "I prefer flying at a slower speed." More laughter.

Their talks ended when this man walked to them with a gun in his hand. "Give me all your money." Guss was shocked, reached for his wallet, and handed him the money. He turned to Roger. "Give me your money."

Guss said, "He is deaf." The man poked Roger in the back.

Roger said, "What?"

The robber said, "Money. I want your money." He patted his butt.

Roger stood up and said, "You want me to kiss your butt?"

The man looked at Guss. "What is wrong with him?" That was the second Roger needed. He grabbed the gun and hand, twisted the hand, and pointed the gun at the gunman's head. "Pull the trigger and shoot yourself." Casino police was only a short distance away, but they didn't want any customers to get shot.

The security came when Roger took the gun from him. Roger had a death grip on the man's throat. Security put handcuffs on the man and took the gun from Roger. Guss was only five feet six inches tall. He walked to the would-be robber and kicked him in his crotch. He doubled over for a second.

Guss came up with a right hand and hit him in the mouth, breaking two teeth loose, then ripped his pocket.

"This is my money, you stupid f——r." Guss kicked him again. Security had to carry the man away because he could not walk for a while. City police were waiting outside. The police took him away.

Guss said, "Thank you for your help."

Roger said, "You also helped by telling him I was deaf."

Guss said, "What! you want me to kiss your ass?" The two and several customers around them started laughing also. Guss put his money back in his wallet. The two sat down again and continued their gambling. An hour later, the chief of police came in the casino and found Roger.

He handed him five thousand dollars. "This is the reward money for his capture."

Roger said, "Thank you, Chief. I didn't know he was that bad."

"I don't know why he picked a casino. Most of his robberies were on the street and stores," the chief said. "He still isn't walking." The three men laughed. Roger counted the money and gave half to Guss.

"I couldn't move without you distracting him."

"Thank you, Roger." Guss started talking about his life. "After Korea, I was happy for no more war."

Roger said, "That didn't last did it."

"No. Our squadron went to a carrier and to Vietnam. We took turns blowing up their trails and trucks. Several of us got shot down. I lost two planes on my first trip in Vietnam. One of my rescues was at sea. I only floated for a couple of hours when I was picked up. A petty officer pulled me out of the water. His name is Petty Officer Wilson." He got tears in his eyes. "I would still like to meet him."

Roger said, "I know two Wilsons in Missouri. Both retired petty officer first class. The younger one talked about rescuing several pilots during the Vietnam war. He was the boat engineer."

"Could he be my savior? On my last cruise, I was shot down for my third time. I crashed in the jungle. The VC were on me before I could get out of the plane." He wiped his eyes. "I was a prisoner for two years. I was rescued by a lone person. One mean man. He came into the camp at night and killed nineteen VC, NVA men. He led us to the river, and we waited two days for some patrol boats to come by. We were flown to Hawaii.

Roger said, "I guess I had an easy job. I was base support for my first trip there. My next three trips to Vietnam were on board ships. The last two was on a carrier." Guss and Roger took a break for some food.

Guss said, "I will buy our dinner. Do you know any women looking for a lonely man?" His eyes watered up. The two sat down and ate dinner.

Roger said, "I need a bathroom." Roger got far enough from Guss. He called a young woman he met in Los Vegas. "Manni, do you think you could come up to Reno for a few days?"

"Roger, I will be there in two hours."

"Honey, I love you, but this is not for me. I have been talking to a Navy vet that wants someone to talk to on the long cold nights. He lost his wife several years ago. Do you still want to come up?"

"Pick me up in two hours, honey." Her flight landed, and Roger took her to meet Guss. He was sitting at the bar, about to fall off his stool. Roger took him to his room. Guss didn't have a room here. Manni stayed with Guss. He slept off the alcohol and woke up next to Manni. She had fallen asleep. Roger went to his room to see how Guss was doing.

Roger walked into his room, seeing Guss and Manni talking. Both of them were lonely looking for a good person of opposite sex. The two were laughing. Roger said, "I am happy to see you two are smiling."

Manni said, "Guss, honey, would you be interested in flying to Las Vegas with me?"

"No. I am afraid of flying. It brings back too many bad times when I was a prisoner. I will walk before I fly again."

Manni said, "Sorry, honey. I didn't mean to upset you. Will you ride in a car with me? I have a big, lonely house looking for a man to wake it up."

Guss said, "Okay." The three went to the dealership closest to them by taxi. Manni purchased a three-year-old vehicle. She drove Guss to his rental home, and he packed up his belongings into three boxes. The next morning Manni, and Guss were on their way to Las Vegas.

Guss drove part way to Vegas. The two talked all the way south and very happy for each other's comfort. Manni pulled into the driveway. Guss got very uncomfortable.

"Honey, what is wrong?"

"Is this your house? It's a mansion. I don't know if I can live in such a palace."

"Please, honey, I need your company." Guss stayed but made no promises. Her mom had her own castle across town. Manni would go visit Martha two times a week. Martha was eighty-six years young. Manni was sixty-four. Guss was eighty-seven. The two were very happy together. Roger went back to Missouri.

He talked to Robert Wilson. "I met an older man that was in Vietnam the same time you and your brother were there. He said this petty officer pulled him out of the water after his plane crashed. He had the name Wilson on his shirt."

Rob said, "I must have pulled twenty pilots out of the water. That was our job."

"Does Guss Stevenson ring any bells?"

Robert thought about it for a minute. "A small man, I think. All I saw was Steve. The rest of the name was covered up."

Roger said, "That's him. He said he would like to meet that Wilson."

Rob said, "He was so small I thought, How did he see over the front of the plane?"

"Are you interested in talking to him? He is living in Las Vegas."

"Art, Mary, are you interested in going to Las Vegas for a weekend?"

Both of them said, "No. That is a waste of money." Rob and Roger flew to Los Vegas a few days later. Robert took five thousand dollars with him. His short stories were selling like hotcakes at I Hop. He was making eight thousand dollars a quarter. Charlotte was staying in his house. She had filed divorce papers. He got drunk, went to work, and was fired. In Vegas, Roger took Robert to meet with Guss.

"Is this Guss's house?"

"No. Manni owns the house. I brought two lonely people together."

Manni opened the door. "Hello, honey. Who is your friend?" Guss walked to the door. Robert had his Navy first class petty officer shirt on.

Guss asked, "Are you the man that pulled me out of the ocean?"

Rob smiled and said, "You are awful short. I thought, How can he see over the front of the plane? Yes, I am." The two laughed and hugged each other. Everyone talked for several hours then went to Harrah's casino. Robert wanted to do some gambling. Manni went also. She was playing quarter machines with Roger. The two disappeared for an hour then showed up again smiling.

Guss and Robert went to the dollar slot machines. The two talked about the war while gambling. Robert was doing pretty good. Their slots were progressive pot machines. The jackpot was now up to twenty-six thousand dollars.

Guss said, "I would like to win that pot. Manni is worth six million dollars. I am staying with her for the love of company. When she wants sex, she calls Roger. Mine is dead. Has been for fifteen years. I am eighty-seven. Two years in Korea and six years in Vietnam." Robert forgot to tell security he was packing. Rob stood up because his back was hurting.

Guss said, "Not again." Robert looked in the direction of Guss's sight.

Five well-armed men with semiautomatic weapons. Guss cashed out and moved to the right away from the armed men.

One man fired shots in the air, "Everyone on the floor."

One of the men said, "Stop him and get his money." Rob stepped in front of Guss, pulled his pistol, and fired one shot, dropping the man, turned to the second, fired one shot, and laid him on his back. Guss ran toward the exit. A third man aimed at Guss but didn't fire. He turned to the guest people filling his bag. "Where are Mark and Steve?"

"One of them said they are dead." Robert stepped out from a slot machine and shot the third person.

"Who is doing that?" The last two were sticking together. "Let's get out of here." The last two turned and headed for the exit. Rob was waiting for them, fired two shots dropping both of them. Guss made it to safety outside the casino. Security was over to Robert in a minute when the last one hit the floor.

"You are not allowed to carry a weapon in here."

"Oh, I am sorry. I forgot to tell you I am packing. Let me bring them back to life, then you can deal with them." A very sarcastic voice.

The owner said, "Where did you get your permit to conceal carry?"

"From President Trump two years ago. I helped save his life. My permit is good in all fifty states." The police finally came in and looked at the bodies. The coroner took pictures and removed the bodies. The police had already removed their weapons. The chief came in and talked to Robert. "Where did you learn to shoot?"

"A SEAL team taught me while I was in Vietnam."

"Are you a SEAL?"

"No. I just worked close to their gun range." The local FBI came to the casino then left.

"Can I go back to my slot machine?" Four days later, we were resting at Manni's house.

The FBI came to the door. "Mr. Wilson?" He stood up with his hands out in front. The agent chuckled. "We are not taking you in. The reward for the six robbers is seventy thousand dollars." He was handed a check. "Do you want to work for us?"

"I am seventy-six years old. What can I do? I am retired now and very happy living that way." The casino owner came by the same day a few minutes later. "Thank you, Mister Wilson, for stopping the robbery. This is for you." He handed Robert a briefcase with fifty thousand dollars inside it. An hour later, he was on his way back to Missouri. Char picked him up at the Springfield airport. Guss and Manni were married two weeks after meeting. All three of her boys were working, saving money for their first year of college.

Robert said, "I will help you through college."

JACKI JAMES

Frank had a beautiful wife and three children. Two sons and a daughter. In 1999, he had a nice job working at a mill in Oregon. His weekly pay was good, but he had a drug problem. He was hooked on all drugs: marijuana, cocaine, and heroin. Many friends had tried to help him, but nothing his friends did would help him get off the drugs. He just rejected their help.

In 2005, he was arrested for possession of meth. Jacki was devastated. Her money would stop coming in. She had no skills to work. Married straight from high school, she never worked for pay a day in her life. Jacki didn't know what to do.

Jacki begged the judge, "Please let my husband work during his court appearance for drug possession." Her request was denied.

Three weeks had passed, and no money was coming in. Jacki went to welfare for help. She did get food stamps and used them sparingly. Her life was turned upside down in a very short time. Jacki called her parents but did not get any help. Her parents were two thousand miles away. She was on her own.

She went to a restaurant to see if she could work there. She was hired for a short time to see if she could perform the job.

Jacki did real good and got a full-time position. Her two sons would have to go to day care along with her daughter, Bonnie. She would have some funds left over after paying for day care. That money would be for food and rent. Frank was sentenced to five years in prison. Jacki worked for a year then moved to South Dakota closer to her parents. Her parents let her move in with them. She filed for a divorce and got it.

Jacki's mother, Karen, said, "I will watch over the children while you are working."

Her sons were still young and very active for four- and five-year-old boys. When next September came, James would start school. John was only one year behind him. Bonnie was two years younger than John. With James starting school, most of her wages went to her parents to pay for food and clothes. Jacki was doing good at this restaurant. She even got a pay raise. The tips were a great help for her also. She managed to feed all three for several years.

With both of her boys in school now, Jacki was doing better and much happier. Her ex was out of prison now but not welcome to her new home. He could get messed up on drugs again. All he wanted as long as it didn't include Jacki and her children. Frank came around once but left at the point of a 12-gauge shotgun. He quickly got the hint and was never seen again. Jacki had a good job and was very proud of her accomplishments.

Her boys were now in the third and fourth grades. Bonnie started the first grade. Their grades were very good. Not the top of the class but close to it. Bonnie was in the first grade three months then moved to the second grade. She was very intelligent. She learned to read by watching and listening to her brothers.

Jacki was still working at the restaurant. Surviving was not what she wanted. She was looking for a better job, but with no experience to get that better job, she would be stuck at the restaurant. There were many nights she would cry herself to sleep. Her children were the only things that kept her going. Jacki saved some money and started taking night classes at the junior college eight miles away.

Her third year of classes, she met a young man doing the same as her to get a better job in their future. Jacki and John talked about their future. Hoping to improve their education and find a better job, the two were working during the day and attended the night classes after work. John and Jacki started spending weekends studying together, among other things.

Her mother asked, "Are you two going to get married soon?"

"Mom, we are still without a good-paying job. John lives with friends, and I am doing the same. You and Dad are my best friends." She got tears in her eyes. "I would still be lost if it was not for you and Dad giving me and my children a place to stay." She wiped her eyes. "I love you, Mom, and you too, Dad. I will find some way to pay you back when my school is complete and working full time with better pay."

Mom said, "We appreciate your thoughts, honey, but don't kill yourself getting there."

Dad commented, "We want you in one piece with your sanity intact."

Jacki and John finished their first two years of classes. It took them four and a half years to do it, but now the two had to pick a major subject. John had several ideas, but all required full-time school. Neither one had the money to do that.

Jacki's father said, "Apply for a student loan. You will have to pay them back, but you will be able to get your degree without working your ass off." Everyone laughed.

Her dad said, "Both of you, pick your major and apply for the student loan."

Mom said, "We would love to help you with finances, but we are just surviving with three munchers." She then laughed along with everyone else. James started the eighth grade, John was in the seventh, and Bonnie would start the sixth grade. Jacki and her parents somehow found a way to make sure the children had good clothes as they grew up. John contributed some funds also.

John and Jacki got their student loans and continued college with their third year. John Watkins was working on a degree in business management. Jacki James was working for a finance degree. Their classes went in different directions but stayed close to each other after each day was over. John's apartment was their home and study hall every night. Sunday was a day of rest for their minds. Both of them would spend Sunday with her children and parents.

Jacki and John took turns cooking their meals. Part-time work was needed to buy their food. John was working at Sears part time, and Jacki's part-time job was a waitress. The first semester came to an end, and now, it was time to relax the mind. Christmas was a few days away, and the children would want something for Christmas. John had saved three hundred dollars to get Jacki and her children something.

John bought two baseball gloves for the boys with a ball and a bicycle for Bonnie. John kept the gifts in the spare bedroom until Christmas day, which was still three days away. Jacki purchased a dress for Bonnie and jeans for the boys. She wouldn't tell John what he would be getting. Jacki searched the house but couldn't find the gift for her from John. Her gift was in her parents' house. Karen had it in her bedroom. John paid for her gift a little at a time. Now that both of them were twenty-six, John thought it was time to give her what she really wanted. It was Christmas day, and they went over for breakfast. The children had already opened the gifts from their grandparents. John and Jacki walked in with many gifts. Her kids jumped up and ran to her and John. We passed out the gifts to three happy children.

John went back to the car and brought in a bicycle for Bonnie. Karen went into her bedroom and came out with the gift for Jacki from John. Jacki gave John his gift. He opened the box and looked at a beautiful watch.

She said, "Now you have no reason for being late to anything, especially dinner." Everyone laughed. John stood there for a few seconds then gave her a kiss.

"Thank you, honey. I was going to let you open this, but I changed my mind." He went down to one knee, opened the ring box, and asked her, "Will you marry me and be my wife?" Through her tears, she said yes. John stood up and placed the ring on her left ring finger. The two held each other with several kisses. Karen and Stan were both surprised. Karen didn't know what was in the box. John had put the ring in a larger box to confuse everyone. It worked.

John pulled a package from his pocket and handed it to Stan. "I didn't forget you and your wife." Stan opened the package and looked at John.

"Oh my gosh, John. You need this for school supplies."

"No, this is extra away from the student loan. It is for you for taking care of our children."

Jacki's eyes lit up and gave John a hug. "I love you, sweetie." Karen gave John a hug and kiss and said, "We really appreciate your help." The money totaled three hundred sixty dollars. The snow didn't stop the boys and Bonnie. James and John went outside and started playing catch with two feet of snow on the ground.

Bonnie tried riding her bicycle. After several tries, she managed to ride several blocks and then came back home. She gave John a hug. "Thank you, sir. I love this bike."

Stan said, "Now you two need to set a date set for the wedding."

Jacki said, "After graduation. We need to save for that day." She looked at John.

John said, "I agree."

They went back to their house, getting ready for the next semester. Books were purchased, and classes were set for the spring semester. Working part time, John and Jacki scrimped through the semester and saved 243 dollars. Their grades were not compromised. Jacki's grades were 3.62 average. John was doing good with his GPA of 3.58. His classes were a little harder than Jacki's classes.

Summertime was here. Happy days ahead. Full time work and a lot of saving money for their wedding. The summer was almost gone, and their savings account was now one thousand six hundred sixty dollars. A few more working days, then back to school for their senior year. With books purchased, their classes now in session, there was only part-time work for either one of them.

The fall semester went pretty fast. Both of them had high grades. Another holiday break. James was now in high school, and the two other children were right behind him. The three children received clothes this Christmas. Everyone was happy for whatever they got. Mostly clothes.

Stan asked the wrong question. "John, don't you care about your parents? Why haven't you visited them?" John walked outside and sat on the porch steps.

Stan said, "Oh, crap. I said the wrong thing. I guess I better apologize to him." He went outside and sat down beside John. "I guess I said the wrong thing. Sorry, John."

"It's not your fault. My parents kicked me out after I graduated from high school. I found a job to buy enough food to keep me alive." John wiped his eyes. I was homeless for three years before I got a job that helped me get a rental apartment. Now that I am doing better, I will never forgive them for their actions. Nor will I ever visit them."

"You are shutting them out of your life."

John cut in. "Just like they shut me out of their life." He got up and went for a walk through the snow. Stan walked with him.

John said, "After we graduate, we will find some place that is warmer during the winter." He was laughing now. "This cold weather is killing me."

Stan also laughed. "It takes a long time to get used to it. We have been here thirty-two years now." Back at the house, Christmas dinner was ready. Everyone sat down, and Stan said a payer, then everyone ate dinner. The rest of the day was pretty quiet. Jacki's children were very smart. Their grades were very good.

John and Jacki started their last semester. The excitement was growing in their bodies. The classes seemed easy for Jacki, but John was having a little trouble with his classes. At home after one month of classes, he said to Jacki, "I think I picked the wrong subject. I am having trouble with these classes."

Jacki said, "Don't do any part-time work, and concentrate on schoolwork. We have enough to cover expenses, honey."

John did that. Two more months passed, and it was time for graduation. Both were very excited. Their grades were 3.70 GPA average each. Jacki's parents and her children were there for the graduation. John's parents somehow found out where he was and were there for his graduation.

He saw them and told them, "Get the hell out of my life. I made it on my own. Leave me and my friends alone."

The ceremonies went at the normal pace with several people talking, then there was the process of all the students receiving their bachelor's degree on June sixth. John and Jacki were thrilled. Their marriage date was set for the sixteenth day of June. John and Jacki were ready for their wedding day. Jacki was pulled away for the last four days. John had to cook his own food, but he didn't mind.

The four days passed fast. John allotted one thousand dollars for her wedding dress. His rental suit was only forty-six dollars. The wedding was at the local church on Sunday with the full congregation of churchgoers. Everyone loved the wedding during regular church hours. When the ceremonies were over, Jacki and John left and went to the reception.

Four hours had passed when John and Jacki left and went to their house for a few days. After several days alone, both of them submitted their resumes in a warmer climate. Their children stayed with Grandpa and Grandma. Their trip started in South Dakota and ended in San Diego, California, six days later. Both of them put their resumes out to the local business community. We made several visits to businesses.

Three days were spent looking for a job. They were sitting at home, very discouraged. Jacki fixed supper and then sat down when her phone rang. Jacki was asked to come in to the bank in the morning.

She said, "Yes, I will be there. That was Wells Fargo. I have to go in for an interview." She was really excited and hopeful for a job.

John looked at the phone and said, "Call me, please."

Jacki went in for the interview and started work that morning. She was happy. John continued looking. He made several interviews, but there were no calls yet. One month passed, and he and Jacki talked about him changing his major subject to something else.

She said, "Give it a little more time, honey. Don't give up so soon."

John said, "I can't have you paying all the bills while I sit around doing nothing to help." The next morning, John took Jacki to work then went to the college. He was thinking about a second major. The dean met John in the registry room. "I received your resume from a friend. Our business management instructor wants to retire. Are you interested?"

John hesitated two seconds. "Yes, when do I start?"

"Follow me, John." He followed the dean to the classroom. There he met Mr. Gary Reed.

He looked at John and said, "Do you want my job? You are going to kick me out," then started laughing. "I am sixty-eight now and ready to quit teaching. Have a seat, and I will give you some good instructions."

The two talked for over an hour, then Gary cleared out his desk and told John, "Have a seat. This is your class now. I am sure you will be a good instructor."

John sat and looked at the books. Mr. Reed left and went into retirement the next week. John read several pages of the books. The books were the same ones that got him the bachelor's degree. He knew the four books very well. John sat for a while and made some adjustments to the position of his desk.

John left the college and went to the bank. He walked into the bank, trying to keep a straight face. It didn't work. Jacki asked, "You got a job? Where are you working, honey?"

"I am a teacher now starting next month. I am really happy. We need to get another car."

Her boss, Fred, said, "I have two extra cars. Both of them run real good if you want to check them out this evening." John picked up Jacki after her work and drove to Fred's house. There was still plenty of daylight, so John test drove one of the cars. Jacki took the other for a test run.

John said, "Sorry, Fred, but these are too hard to decide which one is the best."

Jacki looked at John. He smiled. "Which one do you like, honey?"

"You are right, but I like the blue one."

Fred said, "Either car is two thousand dollars. You can make payments Jacki. Just keep a record of payments." She said okay. John put two hundred dollars down. Jacki drove it home. She was happy for the car on payments and happy for John's job. School started in five days. John drove to the school and reviewed the books again. Just two books this semester. The other two books next semester.

John was ready to start his teaching now. His first class came into the room. Only sixteen students. Very low for a class. After the two classes were over, John went to the dean, and the two talked for a while. Fred said, "The class gets smaller each year. I may have to cancel the class next year if there are not more students signing up for the class."

John said, "I came here to sign up for a finance class or something else different."

Fred said, "This subject is an easy one, but the opening positions are very few. You have the afternoon to work on a second major this year. Next year, we may not offer this class again." John signed up for two afternoon finance classes. He studied hard and finished the classes with high grades, 3.84. His business classes were not hampered by his finance classes.

John talked to Jacki when he got home. He told her what he had done and why.

She said, "Good for you, honey. Keep up the good grades." Jacki wanted to go to South Dakota for Christmas. John booked flights for two.

Their flight landed three days before Christmas. She and her children started crying when the kids met their mom.

We purchased some clothes for the children. John gave Stan one thousand dollars and told them about his job maybe coming to an end.

"I am taking finance classes just in case my position ends. I only have to take one full year of classes. Half this year and the remainder next year."

The children really missed their mom and wanted her to stay there.

She wanted to stay also. She checked with the local banks and many other places. The Wells Fargo bank called her for other job. The manager called her parents' home to let her know she was given a position at the bank there in Sioux Falls. She let out a big yell. She scared everyone. "I got a job here at the bank. It is only two miles away. Is that okay, honey?"

"If that is what you want, baby, then you can take the job. I have one more semester to teach, then I can switch to finance field for one more semester."

"I love you, sweetie. I will be good and very happy here. I want you to call often."

"How about on the weekends? I love you too, baby." Christmas day came, and everyone received something for Christmas. Jacki started working two days after Christmas. John stayed through New Year's Day and three more days. He flew back to San Diego for the spring semester.

He kept his promise and called every weekend for a couple of hours. Their baby and her belly was getting larger.

Now five months along, she and John were excited.

John said, "I will be there the day after classes are over. I already have my flight reserved. I miss you, baby."

She said, "I miss you too." Four months passed, and school was out. The next day, John arrived at the airport. Stan was waiting for John. He drove John home. Jacki was still at work for another two hours. James just finished his junior year of high school.

Jacki arrived home and was very happy to see him.

John said, "The spring semester only had twelve students. Fred said there will not be a class next year."

Jacki asked, "What are you going to do now, honey?"

"I got another offer. The Las Vegas mafia is looking for an accountant." Then he started laughing.

"You brat. You scared me."

"I will be taking one more semester, then I will be a certified accountant, finance officer."

Bonnie asked, "Is that some kind of a cop?"

"No, honey, it is a position in the finance field. Like my job."

John said, "I will finish the classes here. We need to go back to San Diego, sell our house, and move everything up here. I will not stay there without you, sweetheart. I need to find another teaching job or my pay will stop."

Jacki said, "Check with the schools to see if there will be any openings come September. Most of the staff is still at school." John went to several schools in the local area first. He left a copy of his resume and would wait for a call. He also visited the college. There was one opening, for a math teacher. He requested to be on the substitute teacher list.

Jacki and John flew back to San Diego with James. He would help drive back to their home. John rented a U-Haul truck and a tow dolly. The house went on the market. The realtor had an offer before John and Jacki could get everything moved out.

The young couple asked, "Would you please leave the refrigerator and some furniture? We have nothing." Their bed was going with them. They left the items the wife would like for them to leave for them. The young couple finished their second year of college. They packed everything else and waited for a few days to sign the papers to transfer the title. The couple's parents helped them with the down payment.

On the road now, they were on the driving for four days and nights. The fifth day, they were home. Stan and Karen had spent several days looking for a house for John and Jacki.

Stan said, "We were looking in the wrong places. The house two doors down is for sale." They walked down to it and looked outside the house. They talked to the owners and got to look inside. A nice four-bedroom, two-bath house with a large backyard. It was within their budget.

We made our offer. It was accepted. We put twenty-five thousand dollars down and financed the other one hundred thousand with the Wells Fargo finance department. John received a call from the college to teach business management. John chuckled to himself then said he would be happy to teach the class. He went over to the college and talked to some of the staff. The former instructor retired earlier before the year was over. He had a mild heart attack.

John and Jacki got moved into their house along with their children and a new baby girl, Shelli. The college had a full class, thirty to thirty-four students every year for the next seven years.

JEANNA POOL

A young girl still in elementary school. Some of the sixth-grade class students were sometimes mean to her. She was not very good-looking, a ways from pretty. Jeanna was tired of being harassed by the other girls in the class. She skipped school and went for a walk. To where, she didn't care. She walked for a couple of hours, found a place to rest, and sat down on the grass. She started crying. Going back to school was not an option. She hated this school and the students.

While sitting on the grassy hill and crying, a young man heard her sobbing. He followed the sound of sobbing and found her. He didn't say a word, sat down beside her, and took her left hand. He held her for a minute then asked, "What is wrong?"

She said, "I am ugly. No one wants to talk to me."

"I am talking to you. My name is David. What is your name?"

She stopped crying and said, "I am Jeanna."

"What grade are you in. Let me guess, fourth grade?"

"I wish. Maybe I could start over. Sixth grade. What do you do? Did you escape from school too?"

He laughed. "No, I graduated last year from college. I have a degree in cosmetology. I see what your problem is, and I can help you if you want my help. If not, then I will leave."

"What can you do for this ugly face and body?"

"Whatever you want. It is not black market. I work for a reputable firm. I was on my walk for my daily exercise, then I heard some crying."

"Can I believe you, or are you a predator?"

David stood up and pulled a business card from his pocket. "Come over any time." The business was about a half mile away.

Jeanna said, "I passed there on my way here. Are you going back to work?"

"Yes, follow me if you want some help."

She followed him to the business, went in, and talked to the receptionist. The owner, Jerry, came out and talked to Jeana for a few minutes. She needed her face cleaned of all the pimples and needed to lose about ten pounds of fat. Some on the legs, but most was around her waist.

"I am only twelve years old. My mom can't afford any changes to my body. Thank you, but I will have to live with my body."

Dave said, "You have a beautiful body under what we have seen."

Jerry said, "This will be a free advertisement for our business. Are you interested?"

She got tears in her eyes. "Yes. How long will the changes to me take?"

"Not long, maybe two weeks," Jerry said. "We need to take some pictures of your problem areas. Then the 'after' pictures."

Dave said, "We need your parents' permission. Will you talk to them? Bring them here, please."

Two days later, Jeanna and her mother, Joana, walked in the office.

Mary, the receptionist, said, "Welcome, Jeanna, this must be your mother."

She said, "Yes, I am Joana. I understand you can help her complexion at no cost to me."

Jerry and Dave came out of the back room. David said, "We were hoping you would come back. Yes, ma'am, we were discussing what we need to do for your daughter. Where is your husband?"

"He left years ago." Nothing else was said.

"Ma'am, are you interested in some help on your body also? We need some references. Mother and daughter would be a great help for our business," Jerry said.

Dave added, "No nude pictures. Just the areas that need changing. The face, waist, and thighs."

Jeanna looked at Mom. "Can I have these changes, please?"

Her mom said, "Yes, honey. Don't cry."

"I am tired of this face. I have wished I could rip it off and see someone better-looking under there."

"You don't need to rip it off. We can change your looks and retain the best part of what you have," Jerry said.

David said, "Ma'am, you need a little work on your face and some on your legs. Can we do the work on both you and your daughter?"

"When do you want to start? Will I miss any work?"

"We can wait for your days off and no work missed."

"I am off for the next two days starting tomorrow. Jeanna can miss as many days as she wants."

David said, "I know. She told me all about the classmates teasing her all the time for being ugly."

"Mom, after this is done, I want to go to a different school. I hate those students. Those girls are so mean. Their favorite name for me is Cesspool."

Dave said, "Just wait for a while, Jeanna, then decide if you want another school." Jeanna went in the back room for some pictures. Joana followed. Jerry took some pictures of her bad areas also. Joana was off work for the day, so Jerry started with her. A freeze process to remove the fat from the thighs. She was told the body would expel the fat. The freeze would kill the fat cells. Joana lost six pounds in thirty minutes. Jeanna had four pounds removed from her middle.

"Your legs will feel very cold, but the removal of fat will not hurt your body," Dave said.

The next day, Jerry started working on Jeanna's face. He said, "This solution will dry up the acne and wipe it off. No squeezing it out. The spots will heal themselves, and you will have a nice and smooth complexion. This procedure will take several applications over a week or more. It all depends on how bad the problem is."

Dave used the same solution on Joana's face. She was not that bad. Maybe three days. She could come back after her work in three days for the last application. Jeanna would need more days off from school. She refused to go to school. She didn't want any more teasing from those dirty-minded girls.

The freeze sessions had to be a week apart. Joana lost another six pounds on her second session. She was feeling like a woman again. Joana received a lot of compliments on her reduction of her mid-body spare tire.

She said, "I am having it deflated." She and her coworkers laughed. Jeanna finally went to school after three weeks away from school. Her face was totally different. Nice and smooth. No more midriff and thinner legs.

She didn't get any rude words from the "high-class" girls. They just ignored her. She didn't care either way. Jeanna felt better, and her mom was a new person also. She got many compliments from regular customers. Joana was asked out many times in the last three weeks.

She said, "I have things to do, sorry." She did not want to go out with those horny men. One of them she called Horny Forney. His name is Doug Forney. Jeanna finished the sixth grade with a C. She still wanted to transfer to another school.

This city had several schools. Where she lived, there was only one other school she could go to. No busses went that way. Walk or stay where she was. Mom could not afford to take her to the other school, so she went to the seventh grade at the same school. The seventh grade received two new students.

Their teacher said, "We have two new students in our class. Twin girls."

The girls went up to the front on the class. "I am May," one said, and the other said, "I am June."

May said, "I was born eleven fifty-seven p.m., May thirty-first."

June said, "I was born five minutes later, twelve-oh-two a.m., June first." The class erupted in laughter.

May said, "We are happy it wasn't September and October. We have no idea what our names would be."

A student piped up, "Sep and Oc."

June said, "I like my name. I am smarter than May."

"We will see, sis." At their last school, their grades were A+ in all subjects. The twins started talking to Jeana during the recess. She didn't know how to take it. Someone finally was talking to her. She was happy.

Jerry and David's business was doing good. An average of six patients per week now. Jerry was thinking about hiring another cosmetologist. The two talked about the hiring and dismissed the thoughts. The fat freeze was the biggest seller. Six patients a week. One each day now for eight months. They grossed three hundred thousand dollars the first year. Some of the patients were part of their advertisements.

Jeanna and the twins were good friends. Jeanna was really happy and told the twins what had happened to her the last two years at school. The twins looked at each other.

May said yes. The girls took Jeanna to their house. Their father, Mark, and mother, Marji, were third-degree black belts in karate. May introduced Jeanna to their parents. Both of them had a bachelor's degree. He was an electrical engineer, and she had a finance degree.

Jeanna said, "I am happy to meet you. Your daughters are the first two to talk to me in three years." She got tears in her eyes. "I need to go home now. My mom is expecting me for dinner. I will see you in school Monday, okay?"

The girls said, "Yes, Jeanna. Be safe."

Their mom said, "Jeanna, I will drive you home." Marji took Jeanna home and talked to Joana for a few minutes.

When Marji got home, she asked the girls, "What happened to her in school?"

The girls said, "She had a bad acne problem. The other girls called her names and 'ugly girl.' Jeanna said their favorite name is 'cesspool.' Her name is Jeanna Pool. The school would not do anything about the name calling."

Mark said, "I know what you are thinking. No fighting."

"But, Dad," then May laughed.

Marji said, "Those girls should be expelled from school."

"Those girls quit teasing her since she went to the cosmetology office."

May said, "She and her mom were the two first to show what cosmetology can do for a person's complexion in their promotions."

Marji said, "Joana really loved her makeover. She had many offers for dates, but she was not interested. She didn't like those men." There was only two men, but they were working somewhere out of the state. She was hoping one of them would come back."

Jeanna was bringing her grades up. She had an A, three Bs and a B+. The twins were doing everything they could to help Jeanna. The stuck-ups were still that way. May and June started teaching Jeanna karate. It was a slow process. The twins were second-degree black belts. Mark and Marji had been thinking about starting a school in town to teach karate. Their ideas didn't materialize. The town had four karate schools already.

Marji asked, "Jeanna and Joana, do you want to learn self-defense?"

Joana said, "Yes." Every day after work, Joana and Jeanna would go to the Burkes' home and spend some time in the backyard or in the garage when the weather got bad. Their twins were helping also. The whole school year passed, and Joana and Jeanna were third-degree green belts. Two happy women. The two could compete with the other people in their class and win most of the battles. Every loss was another training session.

Summer gave Joana some more training. She was a low-paid cashier at a grocery store.

Marji said, "You need a better job. What do you want to be? The world is out there waiting for you."

"I cannot afford a school to get a degree. I married after high school with plans on going to college to be a nurse. Jeanna came along, and her father decided he didn't want any children. He left before Jeanna's first birthday. If he ever comes back…"

Marji cut in, "You don't want to say any more, Joana."

She laughed. "You are right." Jeanna and her mom went home and fixed some food for dinner.

"Mom, what happened to my father?"

"Maybe later, honey. I don't want to talk about that bastard."

"What will I do if he approaches me, saying he is my dad?"

Joana laughed, "Beat the shit out of him." A sip of coffee. "Honey, he was worthless. When he knew I was pregnant, he beat feet and left me with just you. No home and no job. After you were born, I managed to get a job working in a convenience store." Joana got up and made herself a strong drink. "I hate that man and always will."

"Mom, what hate you have for my dad, that is your hate. I will always love you no matter what we do. I do not know him, and I don't know what he looks like. I guess I am lucky I have you. You could have put me up for adoption but kept me by your side. That is why I love you so much." She wrapped her arms around her mom, and both of them cried. Nothing more was said about her father. School started for Jeanna's eighth grade.

She was really happy. She and her mom went to the cosmetology office and had a great reunion with Mary, David, and Jerry there. They talked for a couple of hours. It was after business hours. Just five more years for Jeanna, and then maybe college. Joana finished her first year of nursing school with very high grades. Now one more year, and she could be a nurse. Her dreams were finally coming true. Jeanna just wanted to graduate from high-school. She had no other plans for her future.

Joana still didn't know who paid for her school. She thought it was Marji, but she found that Marji had nothing to do with her school funds. (The state paid for her school.) The school board knew she wanted to be a nurse so bad she would not fail. The state does this for a person until that person graduates. Then they will find a deserving person for his/ her schooling. Joana had three weeks before her final test. Her studying was many long nights.

The last three weeks passed, and Joana was very nervous but took several deep breaths and walked into the classroom. She found her seat and waited for the test to be placed in front of her. There were twenty-five students there.

One of the younger students said, "What is Grandma doing here?" Joana laughed. The test was put on each desk, and then the word was given to start.

Three hours later, some students took their test up to the monitor's desk.

The mouth said, "Grandma is still trying to read the medical terms." Joana had finished her test in two hours but held it for no special reason. The final word to stop and bring your test up to the desk. That was it. Everyone left the room and would have to wait for the final grades. The next day the class assembled in the test room. The grades were handed out. Sue, the mouth, did pass but only by two points.

She opened her mouth. "How did Grandma do?" She looked at Joana.

The instructor said, "How did you do, Sue? You are the bottom of the list of those that passed. The top person is," he laughed, "Grandma. Sue if you get a job, you will be working for Joana. Her score is 3.98. The top score of all of you."

The other women and men stood up and applauded. "Good for you, ma'am. Do you want a baby working for you?" Everyone laughed, except Sue.

The instructor said, "Joana wanted this degree. If you just want a job, you might not get what you want."

Joana was hired right away at the local hospital. Her pay just increased by threefold. Jeanna finished the eighth grade. Now she was in high school. Jeanna talked to her mom. "Can we move now, Mom?"

"I have a job right here, honey. My pay is three times higher. I don't want to lose my job. I start tomorrow. Please, honey, I am finally getting some money for your college. Don't spoil it. If you want to leave, please don't go. You are the only one I have." Both of them were crying.

"Mom, I will stay with you. Without you, I will have nothing. I love you, Mom."

Joana started her job under instructions with the head nurse. She wasn't sure what field she wanted, but she would get training in several fields. Joana ended up in ER. She was not afraid of seeing blood. Joana now had her position and was very happy. Jeanna started high school. The twins were teaching Jeanna how to study.

The three had the same classes. Jeanna was trying to keep up with the grades of the twins.

Those two girls had the intelligence of their parents. The girls were getting 3.98, and Jeanna was only getting 3.6.

She was told, "Don't try too hard. Just do the best you can. Your grades are exceptional. Don't rack your mind, Jeanna. You are doing just great."

May said, "Most of the other students are close to what your grades are."

June said, "We are different. Don't try to keep up with us. Just do your best, Jeanna." She did listen to the twins and finished her first year with very high scores. 3.65. Summertime and her mom was working a twelve-hour shift. One day shift for two weeks, then a night shift for two weeks. It was hard, but Joana loved it. Many weeks, Jeanna would have to fix her own supper. She was kinda getting used to her mom's schedule. She didn't like it, but her mother was happy, so she would be happy for her mother.

Jeanna spent a lot of time with the twins and learned more about karate. She advanced to second-degree brown belt. Her summer was great. Jeanna met a young man and had a couple of dates with him. She refused to give up her virginity, so those boys went to a girl that would lie down for them. The twins were the same as Jeanna. Keep it as long as possible.

The girls' third year started. The twins had their driver's license. Jeanna had to wait for October. Joana bought her daughter a car. It wasn't a new car, but it was in good shape and ran. Jeanna was happy.

The year seemed to drag on. Every day felt like a week to her. The year continued slowly, but Jeanna made it through to Christmas holidays. Joana had Christmas off this year. Jeanna was happy for that. The two celebrated the day with exchanging gifts. Jeanna worked at a deli on her time off.

The new year brought to the end of her third year of high school.

Jeanna was still working during the summer. She needed the extra money.

Her mother was not rich like the twins' parents. It wasn't much pay, but it was her money. The summer ended, and Jeanna and the twins were on their last year of high school. The three girls were very excited. This was the last year for the elite to get even with Jeanna for getting the twins on her side.

Their attack was planned for the first weekend of the new school year. It would be on all three girls. Seven to three. Quite unfair. The weekend came right after the football game was over. Seven mean girls headed for the exit with vengeance on their minds. The seven girls met the twins and Jeanna away from the crowd. Three minutes later, seven girls were lying on the ground with busted lips and bruised ribs.

Jeanna and the twins found one of the teachers and the football coach. The girls explained what had happened.

The teacher and coach said, "I guess those girls were asking for what you gave them."

The teacher asked, "What did you hit them with?"

Jeanna said, "I have a second-degree brown belt in karate. The twins are both black belts, second degree." The teacher and coach laughed. The teacher called for an ambulance. A few minutes later, the medical crew attended to the injured students.

May drove Jeanna home. The girls laughed about their feat. Jeanna told her mom when she got home. A few days later, this man showed up at their house. Joana was working. Jeanna asked, "Who are you?"

"I am your father." She hit him seven times in five seconds. He went down like a tree falling in the forest. Jeanna called her mother then called the police. Joana and the police arrived at the same time. He was still lying on the ground. Joana and the police just laughed.

"Honey, how many times did you hit him?"

"I don't know, Mom. He said he was my father. That was the last thing I remember. Then I saw him on his back on the sidewalk."

The medics showed up and took him to the hospital to see what damage was done to him.

A couple days later, he left the state and went back to his own world away from hell on wheels, his daughter.

Jeanna graduated from high school with grades high enough to get an academic scholarship in teaching. Jeanna was so happy she didn't know what to do. Joana was there for her graduation. Jeana was stunned and didn't know what to say.

Marji said, "Accept the offer, Jeanna. It only happens once. You will never get this offer again."

Mark said, "Do it, Jeanna."

Jeanna accepted the offer. She had all four years paid for by the college. She went to the college and talked to some staff, and she was assigned a room for her upcoming school years and a meal ticket. The meal ticket was only good during the school year. Jeanna found a job close to the college to feed herself during the summer.

Jeanna was working the evening shift with a young man. He wanted to make money to buy a car. He was only sixteen. This guy came in, looked around, and then came up to the cashier. He wanted change for a twenty.

Jeanna said, "We don't cash bills. We need the money for paying patrons when they make a purchase."

He reached for his right front pocket. Jeanna felt something wrong and, with her fast reflexes, she hit him four time in three seconds, knocking him out. The boy stood there with an open mouth. *What the hell did she just do?* went through his mind. Jeanna called the police. One arrived in less than two minutes. Jeanna went around the counter and looked at the guy on the floor.

The officer came in the store and looked at the man on the floor. He immediately cuffed him. The officer knew who he was. A wanted man who had robbed several stores in the last three months. A one-thousand-dollar reward was offered for information of his whereabouts. The location was evident. He was on the floor with a broken nose and a concussion. The officer made a call. Three more patrol cars arrived.

One officer asked, "Who did this?"

The young man said, "It wasn't me." He didn't want to get in trouble.

Jeanna said, "I damaged his body. He started acting strange. He wanted change for a twenty. I told him we do not change bills without a purchase. He reached for his belt, so I hit him."

The police checked his clothing and found a knife and a .38 pistol.

After checking his prints to confirm his ID, their suspicions were right.

He was wanted by the police. Jeanna was told the reward for him was one thousand dollars. She smiled and said, "Good, I need the money."

Her shift ended after another hour. The next shift came in, and Jeanna went home.

Mom worked the night shift, but she watched the news. Joana heard about it shortly after it happened. The whole episode went viral on the Internet the next day. Joana got home, and Jeanna had supper for her mother when she made it home. She walked in the house, stopped, and looked at Jeanna. "How many times did you hit him?"

"I don't know, Mom. I just know he didn't get up to protest."

Joana started laughing. "You did right to protect yourself and the store employees." A pause. "Be careful, honey. I don't want you to come in to the hospital with a bullet in your body. I just might die right there."

"I will, Mom. I don't want to die for a few dollars. Are you hungry, Mom?" We sat down and ate dinner at 8:00 a.m. Joana went to bed shortly after eating. Jeanna watched the local news then went outside so Mom could sleep.

Jeanna had to wait to move into the dorm room, so she was still staying at home. Mom needed the company. A few days later, Jeanna went to the police station and received her reward. She took the check to the bank and opened her own account. Jeanna went to work again the next day.

Her boss said, "Thank you, Jeanna, but please do not get hurt. Your life is not worth losing over a few dollars."

Jeanna's first year was about to start. She stopped working the day shift. Her boss helped Jeanna start a light work schedule, plus extra hours on the weekend after schoolwork was finished. The twins went to a different state for their college. Jeanna had registered for six classes on her first year.

She was doing pretty well on her first semester and was working at the convenience store. She worked four hours each day, from 4:00 to 8:00 p.m., then she would rush to her room and finish her homework. A shower and then some sleep. It was a busy schedule, and she was keeping her grades up also. November was here, and the weekend came. She could relax for a day.

A trip to the convenience store for her four-hour shift. She walked in to see the place being robbed. The gun-toting man pointed his gun at her. "Get over here, give me your purse."

"I don't carry one, just to piss off any robber."

"Get down on the floor."

"All I want is some coffee. I will only be a minute, then I will be gone." She pointed to the coffee. The man shot a round into the ceiling. That instant change of the gun's direction was all she needed.

Jeanna moved so fast the robber could not react fast enough to stop her. She was only two feet away. Jeanna grabbed his gun hand, the right hand, and with her right arm, she hit him, breaking his nose, knocking him out. She also broke his right hand, causing him to drop the gun. The cashier pushed the alarm and called the police.

The police were there in three minutes. The first officer came in, looked at the man on the floor, and looked at Jeanna. "You again." Then he laughed.

"His gun is over there," she said, pointing to it. The officer went over and bagged the pistol. Another officer put the handcuffs on the attempted robber. Jeanna started her shift, and the other cashier went home very shook up. He quit working there. The evening shift came in. Jeanna was still there when the owner came in.

The owner said, "We will close up at dusk. I don't want any more robberies. I am selling this place. Jeanna, sorry, but I cannot handle any more robberies. The doors will be closed tonight not to open again." Jeanna would use that time to do more studying for the next test.

The first semester ended, and Jeanna went home for the holidays.

Her mom was happy to see her. "Quit trying to be a hero, honey. I don't want to lose you." She held Jeanna. "Stop it."

"I quit working there. The owner is selling the store."

"Are you hungry? Supper is ready." Jeanna set the table for two and sat down to eat with a lot of talking.

Jeanna talked about her classes. "So far, the classes are pretty easy. My grades are very high, 3.66 average." A pause to take a bite. "I guess I will have to find another job next summer." She and Mom finished eating, cleared the table, sat down, and talked for a while. Joana was working the night shift. She left shortly after eating.

Jeanna sat down in the living room and watched the evening news then looked for a program to watch. Nothing, so she turned off the TV and listened to the music on the radio. She woke up when the front door opened. Her mother just got home. Jeanna looked at the clock. "Oh my gosh, I fell asleep listening to the radio." The sun was up, and Joana went to bed.

Jeanna went to a store to get out and let Mom sleep. She did some window shopping and found a nice sweater. She bought it. When she got home, her mom was up. "I couldn't sleep. I am going to find a daytime job, honey. These shifts are too much on my body."

"Mom, what will you do?"

"I can work for a clinic of the main hospital. Those places only work five days a week. Weekends off and only daytime hours."

"Oh, Mom, I hope you can get one of those positions. Then I can come and visit every weekend." Jeanna chuckled.

"Honey, I would really appreciate seeing you on the weekends."

Jeanna finished her second semester. Her first year. Summertime and Jeanna was home every day. Joana found a clinic that accepted her experience. The clinic was further away from home, but the distance was not a problem. Joana was so happy for her new workplace she almost cried but held it back. She was older but not the senior nurse. Joana didn't care.

Jeanna started her second year of college. This year went very fast. She finished the year with a grade average of 3.70. Her grades were getting better. Her new part-time job was working for Walmart. She worked her way up to a cashier. The pay gave her more money in her account while still in school. The second summer, the twins came home and paid Jeanna and her mother a visit. Jeanna was so happy she cried when she saw the girls.

Joana and Jeanna were invited over for the Fourth of July party. Neither one wanted to miss this, so on the fourth, Joana and Jeanna were there at the Burke residence with some appetizers.

Marji said, "You didn't have to bring anything, Joana. We have so much." The Fourth of July party was great. The Burkes invited several friends from their work. Joana and Jeanna felt out of place. The twins made it better for them.

The girls talked about their high school days and had everyone laughing. The Pools felt better. Jeanna was asked about her job at the convenience store.

"I don't work there anymore. It was fun and scary. That part was when I knocked those two people out for trying to rob the store."

Jeanna was now in her third year of college. Each year, her grades got better. The end of her third year, she had moved up to an average of 3.72. She was so happy. The summer was spent at home with her mother. She went back to Walmart on a daytime shift. Jeanna met a lot of young customers. Many men were interested in Jeanna.

"I am at work now. After work, I go home and spend the evening with my mother."

Her last year started, and she was so excited. The last two semesters were just around the corner. Jeanna called May. The girls exchanged phone numbers during the first year even though they were two thousand miles apart. Jeanna and Joana still loved the twins and their parents. That is the best family either one had met. Rich but not a stuck-up attitude.

At the fourth party, the twins told Jeanna and Joana their parents' past life.

"Our parents were dead broke while trying to get through their first year of college. Mom and Dad managed to complete their four years while working two jobs each." Joana and Jeanna respected the twins' parents for fighting their way through college working extra jobs to feed themselves. That is why the Burkes were willing to help Joana and Jeanna.

The Burke parents showed up for their daughters' graduation from college. The girls received their bachelor's degree. May followed her mother. A finance degree. June got her degree in psychology. Their graduation was a week before Jeanna's graduation. The Burkes showed up to watch Jeanna receive her bachelor's degree. Jeanna almost cried when she was handed her diploma. Her final grades were 3.90. Her grades surprised the Burkes and her mom.

Jeanna applied for a teaching position at a local school. She is now teaching English at the high school she graduated from.

LANA

A beautiful girl at birth, her parents gave her the name Lana. She was born on June 23, 1988. Six pounds, nine ounces, seventeen inches, and a very active baby. Before being born, she kicked the crap out of her mother's belly.

Sarah said, "If she keeps this up, I will cut her out myself."

Michael said, "Be patient, honey, just three months left and then we can spank her daily." Both of them laughed. The three months passed, and finally, Lana saw the light of day. Sarah was very happy to have their little girl born.

Before the doctor could spank her, Sarah said, "Let me do that." The doc moved Lana close to Mom. She swatted her butt. Lana started crying.

Michael laughed. "I get the next one."

The doc asked, "Was she that bad?" Another two days in the hospital, Michael took Lana and his wife home. Sarah was out of work for three months. After getting a day care to accept a baby, she was able to go back to work. Lana grew up fast. She started school and did good. She skipped the first grade with her parents' homeschooling. Lana excelled through school. Lana was sent home for fighting while in the sixth grade. Her mom yelled at her, then she asked, "Did you win the fight?" Sarah smiled.

"Yes, Mama, I did beat her butt good. She tried to steal my boyfriend." When her father got home, he scolded her for fighting.

"If you lose one boyfriend, there are a dozen more waiting in the wing." In high school, she had two boys wanting to date her. Lana didn't like either one of them. Her first boyfriend moved to another town.

98

After high school, she went into college. She wanted to be an accountant. After the first year, Lana changed her mind. She wanted to be a teacher.

"Mom, what should I do? I cannot decide on what major I want."

"Well, honey, when you were younger, you thought about being a policewoman, then a boxer. You did good in the sixth grade." The two laughed. "You have one more year to decide, honey." Lana finished her second year of college. At five feet nine inches and pretty tall for a girl, she made her parents very angry. She joined the Navy.

During boot camp, she learned fast on how to protect herself from the "elite." Those girls thought they were better than the rest. The biggest woman said some things bad about Lana.

She just smiled. "You are just jealous that you aren't bad like me."

The fight started, and Lana knocked the woman out with three hits. She took karate classes during high school. She made third-degree brown belt. The "elite" stayed away from her. The company commander had watched the short fight. She didn't say a word to anyone. She, Chief Davis, brought everyone to attention and took them for a short run of three miles the next morning.

"Now if you want to fight, do it here in the desert." Everyone was to tired. The jog back to the barracks wore everyone out. There were no more fights. The company had daily classes and spent some time in the pool to learn water survival. No one drowned. Back to classes and then finished up boot camp training. Lana went to the personnel office in San Diego. She broke a man's finger for grabbing her butt. He won't do that again.

Two years in San Diego, and taking classes at the college, she finished her third year. Lana decided she wanted to be a finance officer.

She was transferred to dispersing office as a third class.

Her chief said, "This will help you get your degree." Lana spent her last two years in dispersing. She did get her degree and left the Navy as a first-class petty officer. She went home and started looking for a job. Her parents and siblings were happy to see her back home. Lana started working for a bank in her hometown.

"Mom, I got a shower, dried off, and looked at my back side. How long has that handprint been on my butt?" Her mom and dad looked at each other and fell down laughing. Lana remembered what her dad said many years earlier. She was joking with her parents. Her dad got to swat the next baby, their son. Lana had two brothers and a little sister. Manny would be going into the seventh grade.

Lana worked for the bank for three years with no pay raise. She put her resume out for higher pay. She got higher pay at a finance company. Her work was auditing. She didn't like that but did her job as requested. She didn't like this job although it was higher pay. Lana did some shopping around for a different job. Three years with the finance business, and she found a better job.

She went to Las Vegas for her next position. That job lasted three weeks. She didn't want to work for the mafia. She was almost killed for leaving but was let go without threats. She found a bank in Texas. Work was great for her. The pay came much higher, but loneliness rolled in, and she almost went home. She had several admirers, but she was still not happy. Lana took a week off and went home.

Virginia was so much better, but the pay was much lower. *What do you choose? Money or love of family?* She went back to Virginia before the fall leaves started falling. Love overruled money. Lana was back home with family. Her parents and younger siblings were happy to see their big sister again. Lana started working for a local bank and stayed with them. Her parents and siblings were very close by.

Lana was dating a man just a year younger than her. He was very nice and honored her thoughts. He never forced himself on her. After two years of knowing each other, he proposed to her. She thought about it for five point three seconds. "Yes!" was her answer. Allen placed an engagement ring on her finger, and the two exchanged several kisses. Three weeks later, their wedding took place at the church close to home.

Lana was pregnant three weeks after the marriage ceremony took place. She and Allen were very happy. This was a first for both of them. Allen and Lana had never been married before. Their new world was in the making with Lana's first child on the way. Allen got home and saw Lana talking to herself.

"Baby, are you all right? You are talking to yourself."

"I am fine. I love you so much. I was talking to our babies."

"What. Did you say babies? How many?"

"Just four. I am kidding, honey. Just two, sweetie. I do not know the sex of them yet. Maybe next month. I hope these two are not like I was with my mother. She wanted to cut her belly and pull me out. I guess I did too much kicking." Allen was doing good with his job as an account. Lana was also happy, but being eight months along, she took the time off to hold onto her babies.

Her water broke, and Allen rushed her to the hospital. Almost an hour passed before their first baby came out. Their first girl was born. Three minutes later, their second girl was born. Allen was disappointed.

"Where is my son? This can't be. Both girls?"

"Honey, next time, I will give you a son."

Their daughters gave them plenty to do to keep up with them. Allen got choked up every time it was his turn to change a diaper. He didn't want any more children. Their girls were walking now, and Lana had another baby in the hanger. Allen kept asking, "Is this my son? Please, honey."

"I will know in a few weeks, sweetie." Three weeks later, Lana came home from the monthly ultrasound look at the baby. Honey, I do not know what you are doing, but you have your sons."

"Did you say sons? Plural?"

"Yes, honey. Two sons this time. This will be my last children. I don't want any more twins. One at a time is enough, but two at a time?" Lana gave birth to two boys this time. Shortly after birth of the twin boys, she had her tubes tied. Two sets of twins were enough for her. Each set hurt her very much on delivery of each baby. She didn't want any more. Each of the children got a good swat from Mom when born. A different doctor.

Lana took some time off to take care of their sons. The girls were four years old when the boys were born. The girls were in school now, the first grade for them. Lana did some home schooling, but neither one skipped the first grade. With the girls in the fifth grade and their boys in the first grade finally, Lana was able to work full time at the bank.

Several years passed. Allen was stopped by the police. He was very intoxicated. Lana didn't know why. He didn't drink at home. He never came home with booze on his breath. *This must be a mistake,* she thought. Lana went to the police station to see what had happened.

Allen had a relapse for some reason unknown. He would not say. She bailed him out and took him home. After several hours talking, she found he was depressed from his past. It caught up with him. He had a bad childhood and it put him down. After several weeks of rehabilitation, he was back to a normal person. He went back to work and was doing better.

Their children were worried about their dad. He was much better now. He kept thinking about his children and the other family members that loved him. The top of his list was his wife, Lana. Back at work for both of them, everything was better. Their children were doing very good in school. As and Bs in all classes from all four children. Allen went to a different company. His pay went up ten dollars an hour.

Lana was hoping for a pay raise. She sent her resume out to the local community. With six hundred thousand people, there should be some company out there that needed a good accountant. A month passed before she got a call.

"Is this Lana Dean?"

"Yes, I am she. Whom am I talking to?"

"I am from J& J. We need a good accountant."

"Yes, I will take it."

"Lana, I haven't told you your duties or your pay yet."

"I don't care. I don't like my present job." She left work in the middle of the working day and went to the company. She talked for two hours and left with a new job. Her new pay would be twenty-three dollars an hour. She was thrilled with the pay raise. A week later, Allen received a pay raise and a supervisor position. His pay was twenty-two dollars and fifty cents an hour.

Matti

Born in Joplin, Missouri, she grew up a very intelligent girl. She was born on August 3, 2025, seven pounds, five ounces, and seventeen inches. She graduated from high school on May 16, 2042. She moved out of her parents' house into an apartment complex in Joplin. Her work was in a restaurant as a waitress. Her rent was low, so she had time to relax and not take two jobs. After four years working there and now twenty-one, she had some extra money.

Matti wanted to have some fun, and so she went to the closest casino in Oklahoma. Her gambling was not going good, so she moved to another one-armed bandit. She sat down by a young man and tried her luck with the quarter machine. She quickly went through her money. With enough cash left, she said, "I'm hungry, what about you?"

Robert said, "Yes, I am too." The two got up, cashed out their tickets, went to the restaurant, and ordered lunch.

"My name is Matti."

"I am Robert. What do you want to eat? I will buy our food." Their talking started before, during eating, and after their food was gone.

Matti asked, "Do you have a room here?"

"Yes, I do. What's on your mind?" She smiled. Up in his room, Matti needed the bathroom. A few minutes had passed, and both were in the shower. Matti washed all his hair. It was almost six feet long. Just a couple of inches from dragging on the floor. Robert was six feet, one inch. Matti was six feet tall. While in the shower, Matti lost her virginity. Both were very happy. Five hours in bed and they finally got up for supper.

Back to his room, and finally the sun came up. Rob and Matti got dressed and went down to the restaurant for breakfast. While eating, this drunk came up behind Robert and grabbed his hair.

He said, "Giddy up, pony, giddy up." Rob stood up and hit him, breaking his nose. He fell down but got up again. Before Robert hit him a second time, Casino Security got to him first and led him out of the casino. Rob and Matti went back to his room. The sun woke them up. Time for breakfast again. The two had missed supper the night before. After eating, the two went to the room and showered again. She spent a half hour braiding his hair in two braids.

"I have to get to work now. Follow me home, please." Rob followed her but got sidetracked when that former drunk tried to ram his pick-up. He missed but wasn't going to give up. Matti called the police while driving her car. One officer was close by. He joined the road-rage drunk and pulled him over at a housing project. Rob had a bent rear bumper.

The officer said, "File a suit against him."

"Do you think he will ever pay?"

"He will have to or go to jail for a year."

"That won't help me if he is in jail." Matti went to work and started her evening shift. Rob went to the Dodge dealer and requested a rear bumper.

"We will order it for you."

"I live close to Springfield." The parts man called Corwin dealership and had them order the rear bumper for Rob's truck. He was in love with Matti. He went to the jewelry store and looked at several Ring sets. His jacket opened, exposing his pistol. The store manager pulled his pistol from under the counter.

Rob looked at the gun pointed at him. He reached into his shirt pocket and removed his conceal carry permit and handed it to the manager. He looked at it and asked, "Are you related to the short story writer?"

"No. I am the writer. I am not here to rob you but to buy a ring for a special woman to me. I will not continue without Matti."

Tom said, "Matti Davis?"

"Yes. Do you know her?"

"She comes in here looking at the rings. She likes that one. It costs five thousand dollars."

"Thank you. I will get that one." Robert paid for it and purchased a wedding band for himself. After Rob left, Tom called his brother, Steve.

"Go to the restaurant your daughter is working in and order supper. Hurry, please. I will meet you later after I lock up the store." Steve and Cathy went there and ordered supper.

"We need a night out once in a while, Matti."

"Okay, Dad, Mom. What do you want to eat?"

"Just coffee for now." Rob took his time getting to the restaurant. He wasn't sure if Matti would accept him in marriage. He was real nervous when he walked in. The receptionist asked, "Are you alone?"

"Yes, for a few minutes. She will be here soon." Becky showed him to a table and gave him a menu. He was ten feet from Matti's parents. He sat down and saw Matti with two plates in her hand. She looked at Rob and smiled.

Rob stood up then went down to one knee. She put the plates on an open table, jumped over another table, and landed in Rob's arms. "Yes!" He was on his back now with Matti on top of him.

"I haven't asked you yet. Will you marry me?"

"You know I will, baby. I love you so much. Yes, yes." Rob placed the ring on her finger, lying on his back.

Her mom said, "Honey, let him get up." Tom walked in and saw Rob under Matti. Tom helped them up.

"What did I miss?"

Steve said, "An eagle flying across the room." All the patrons were applauding and laughing about Steve's words.

The manager said, "Watch the news." All eyes went to the TV. It showed Robert going down on one knee and Matti clearing the table and landing on Rob. Tom applauded and also laughed.

The newscaster said, "I think she loves him."

The news people applauded also. "Congratulations to the couple."

Her mom said, "Honey, is that our food?"

"Sorry, Mom. I will get it. Do you want it reheated?"

Dad said, "Quit jumping over tables."

"Mr. and Mrs. Davis, I didn't know who you were. I am Robert."

"We know who you are, but Matti, do you know who he is?"

"Yes, Dad. He is the man I love very much."

"Take care of your customers, honey. We will talk later."

"Don't scare me, Dad."

"It is not bad, honey." She had three tables waiting for their food. After giving them their food, "I have a few minutes."

Mom asked, "When is your shift over, honey?"

"Another half hour, Mom." Matti attended her tables and cleared them when all the customers were gone. She got extra tips for this night. Matti's parents and uncle were the only people in the restaurant who knew Robert's true identity. Matti finally finished her shift and set down with Rob and her parents. Uncle Tom was close to their table.

Tom said, "Are you sure you want to marry this man?"

"Now you are scaring me."

Her mom said, "I see that you don't know much about him. Did you ask him what he does for a living? What is his income like?" She looked at Rob.

He said, "I am a writer. I write short stories for a living. My grandpa started writing years ago. He wrote fifty short stories. After a four-year delay, I continued his wishes, and I have written sixty more short stories."

"Robert, what are you worth right now?" Steve asked.

He thought for a minute, then said, "I think I just went over fifteen million dollars." Matti fainted. Her father caught her before she fell off the edge of the booth seat. A damp cloth on her forehead woke her up.

"Why didn't you tell me, honey?"

"If I told you, you might have turned me down, saying, 'I am not good enough for you.' If you change your mind—"

"That won't happen, sweetie." She held Rob's arm.

"You two need to set a date," her mom said.

Rob looked at Matti. "A week from tomorrow?" Matti said yes.

Tom said, "Go home, Robert. We will see you next Saturday?"

"I will be here, honey." She kissed him, and Rob stood up. "Here is money for her wedding dress." He handed her mother five thousand dollars. Rob went home for an agonizing and nervous seven days. "What if she changes her mind? I hope not." Robert had his suit and went to the church her parents selected then rented a motel room for the day.

The next morning, Rob went to the church. The priest moved him to a back room for a while. The congregation started coming in and got their seats. The two front row seats were taped off.

A man, John, asked, "What is this about? That is my favorite seat." The Davis family came in and sat down in the front row.

John smiled. "I think this a wedding party," he said, talking to his wife.

The priest came out and started talking. "We are blessed today. A young couple will be exchanging vows this morning." He smiled. "No rice inside the church. It took two weeks to clean out the first and last time rice was used in here." Robert was escorted out to the priest and stood there. The priest looked at the organist.

She started playing as Matti and her father, Steve, walked down the aisle. Robert looked at her with awe. She looked so beautiful in her wedding dress. The walk took too long for Robert. Their vows were exchanged as the rings were placed on their ring fingers.

"I now pronounce you husband and wife. You may now kiss the bride." Robert handed the priest a note.

"Please face the guest. I am proud to introduce you to Mr. Robert and Mrs. Matti Wilson." Matti took Rob's arm, and the two walked down and sat down on the groom's side first row. They stayed for the church services. They left right after the last song. Their limousine was waiting for them. There were several bags of rice outside the church. They were covered with rice, then they entered their ride.

The newly married couple were out of sight for five days.

Matti asked, "What do we do now?"

"How about a trip to Hawaii for a week?"

"That sounds boring." She smiled. "When do we leave?" Matti put her arms around Robert. "I love you, sweetie."

"I love you too, baby." Their trip to the Islands was a great pleasure for them. Plenty of time in the ocean water and fresh water pools. Rob and Matti were there two weeks and visited all the Islands. The trip to Los Angeles was nice. Their next stop was Ogden, Utah, to see how his house was. A week there and then home to Niangua, Missouri.

Matti was getting bigger. She is now seven months along.

"Honey, we need to find a house in Springfield. If my water breaks here, you will have to deliver our son on the road. I don't feel safe here."

"You are right, honey. We will start looking in the morning." The two looked at thirty or so houses. Matti finally found the right one just three blocks from the hospital. We bought the four-bedroom, two-bath house. The house was unfurnished. It was $185,000 for the house and another $6,000 for furnishings. After moving in, they just relaxed until Robert rushed Matti to the hospital. Their son was born on September 2, 2048.

At fifteen months old, David was running all over the house now with Matti or Robert chasing him. "Sweetie, it's time to work on our daughter. Are you ready?"

Rob smiled, "I am always ready." They went to her parents' home to visit. "Mom, I am carrying your granddaughter. Are you ready for another grandchild?"

Mom said, "Do I have a choice?" Then she laughed. "When do you expect her birth?"

"First week in September. Dad, Mom, I am very excited for another child." Back on their ranch for a few months, then back to their other home in Springfield for the last month. Their little girl was born September 3, 2050. Matti's parents were there to see the birth of their second grandchild. Steve and Cathy were thrilled. Back at the ranch three months later, Matti said, "Baby, I want two more children."

NANCEE ZEEK

Nancee and her parents transferred from Los Angeles to San Diego, California. Her father's job ended, so he went to work in the naval ship yard. John and Sara Zeek received some severance pay. Their house was a two-bedroom rental. Their only child was Nancy Zeek. She was a junior in high school. Los Angeles was a rough neighborhood to live in.

Nancee was able to protect herself. She cleaned the karate class room after hours to get lessons on self-defense protection. From ten years old to the start of her junior year. Her dad's job closed down, so the family moved to San Diego, where he got another job. While living in Los Angeles, Nancee managed to advance to second-degree black belt in karate.

Nancee only missed three days of school in the transfer. Sara got a job working in a beauty shop close to the base. She did get transferred to the base salon as a stylist. A little more income to help them survive. Their rent and other bills gave them enough to get by on their needs of food and some new clothes now and then.

Nancee met Ted Bensen and talked a lot on their off time. Break time before lunch, two boys sneaked into the girls' bathroom. Seven toilet seats were covered with saran wrap. After lunch, many girls ran to the bathroom. Many screams were heard in the hallway. With wet clothes from urine, some girls left school and went home to change clothes.

Nancee knew who did that dirty trick. Her clothes were still dry but was not happy for the other girls. She came out of the bathroom saw the boys. With two quick strikes, both boys had a shiner on their left eye. She then grabbed them and took them into the girls' bathroom. She said, "Now clean up your mess." One of the girls had to poop. It was sitting on the saran wrap. That girl went to the girls' shower room to clean up then went home.

She yelled at them, "Clean that also. You caused this mess, now clean it up." The maintenance man stood outside the girls' bathroom with a smile on his face. Ted was outside the bathroom when Nancee walked out. The two boys walked out also.

The maintenance man said, "I bet you won't do that again," then he laughed. One of the boys was looking a little green.

The two boys were expelled for a week.

Ted asked, "What did you hit them with?"

"A second-degree black belt in karate."

"Nancee, do you want to work for the next step and get a third-degree black belt?"

"We can't afford any more classes. I guess I will live with my second-degree black belt. Do you have one, Ted?"

"Yes, mine is a third-degree black belt. Also karate. I can help you get the next step. My parents and I are senseis."

"Ted, please don't lie to me."

"I'm not lying, Nancee. Come over to our school and talk to us. I will find a way to help you make the next step." After school was out, Nancee went with Ted to the karate training room.

His mom said, "Hi, son. Who is your friend?"

"This is Nancee. This is my mother, Clair, and my father, Ted Senior. Mom, Dad, Nancee transferred from Los Angeles with her parents. She has a second-degree black belt and wants to finish her third-degree black belt in karate."

Ted Senior said, "You came to the right place. We are both fourth-degree black belts. We trained Elvis years ago. He had to go to another sensei to get his fifth-degree black belt."

Mom said, "We are happy with just a fourth degree. Come in tomorrow, and we can get started for you to advance up one level."

Saturday came and went. No Nancee. Ted met her in school on Monday. "Nancee, honey, why didn't you come over? I waited for you."

"I don't have the money for more classes. We are not very rich. I would like to get the next level, but my parents can't afford it. We are on a shoestring budget."

"Okay. I will talk to my parents tonight." Friday came, and another week of school ended. Christmas was a week away.

Ted said, "My parents will give you two days free just to see if you are ready for the third-degree black belt in karate. Okay, honey?"

"I will talk to my parents. Maybe next year I can find a job and pay my way for a third-degree black belt."

"Nancee, two Saturdays. It is free." A pause. "You are making me angry. Why are you being this way?"

"I am afraid of failing."

"How many times did you fail on your way to your second degree? Probably as many as I did while getting to my third-degree belt. Nancee, honey, give it a try, please." She smiled and gave Ted a hug and a kiss. "Okay, I will be there this Saturday."

Ted laughed. "I know where you live. I will come and get you if I have to."

"Please do that. I have no transportation to get to the karate school." Saturday morning, Ted drove to Nancee's house and picked her up. Ted parked in front of the school. He got out and walked around his car and opened the door for Nancee. She got out, and this man ran up to them with a gun in his right hand.

"Give me your wallet!"

"I will give you my money, but I will not give you my wallet." He grabbed for the wallet, but he was too slow. Ted grabbed his gun hand and pointed it at the gunman's head. A shot was fired. Two officers across the street saw what happened and ran across the street to see the gunman fall to the sidewalk. Ted's parents came outside with fright in their eyes.

Ted said, "He shot himself, Mom."

The officers said, "We saw what happened. Your son protected himself. Is that man dead?"

Ted said, "I don't think so. He just knocked himself out. The bullet just grazed his head."

An officer checked his pulse. "He is still alive." He also placed handcuffs on the man and waited for the medical team to arrive. Nancee and Ted went into the karate class with his parents. His dad chewed him out for thirty minutes. "I don't want to lose you over a few dollars. Don't ever do that again."

"Dad, he was drunk and slow on his reflexes. I saw the opportunity to get his gun hand."

"Don't do that again." Nancee was shook up. Ted had to take her home. He also went home. His parents had to do the training for the young kids. Clair called her son, but he refused to answer the phone. Their karate classes ended early, then they went home. Their son was not at home. TJ went to the beach. He walked all the way out to the Naval air base. The SEAL team was out, running for their daily run.

A member said, "This is our beach. Get off this strip of beach."

Ted said, "I don't see any signs saying that you own this strip." Two SEALS grabbed his arms. Both of them were thrown in the ocean in less than five seconds. Their lieutenant said, "Back off. Finish your running." The two wet team members had some extra weight to pack with them.

Ted walked home and sat on the front porch. His dad talked to him. He apologized for yelling at him. Now he was back in school on Monday and feeling better. He talked to Nancee about what happened.

She said, "Everything happened so fast it scared me. I didn't know you could think that fast. That man died in the hospital last night. The bullet went into his head."

"I am sorry he died. What else can I say?" The rest of the school year went well for him and Nancee. TJ was back, teaching the young karate class students. During the summer, TJ and Nancee started working at whatever job the two could get. This money was for Nancee's college fund. Nancee said, "Teddy, I love you, but I don't have any savings for college."

"Honey, don't ever call me Teddy. That is a fighting word to me."

"Honey, don't you want to be my teddy bear?"

"Well, maybe, but don't ever call me that in school." Nancee got her free classes in karate. After five classes, the day of training came to an end. Ted Senior had all the students line up by age. Ted Junior got his class together and advanced seven students to the next level. Their parents were as excited as the young boys and girls.

Ted Senior and Clair advanced nine students up one level.

Clair said, "I have one more belt." She looked at TJ; he took Nancee's hand and walked her up front. She was surprised. Clair wrapped the belt around her waist as Ted Senior said, "Young lady, you are now a full-fledged third-degree black belt. Congratulations." Nancee was so happy she cried.

The last year of high school for Ted and Nancee started. Two weeks of school was done. The third week started, and the classes assembled in the gym. Several Navy, Marines, Army, and Air Force recruiters were there. Each group of the military talked for a few minutes. One of the SEAL team whispered to his friend, "That is the man that threw me into the ocean." Both of them chuckled.

Their chief asked, "What do you find so funny, petty officer?"

"Nothing, Chief. Do you remember that run on the beach last summer? I just saw the young man that tossed me and Jim into the ocean." The whole school was laughing plus the military people.

He stood up and asked, "Do you want to be a Navy SEAL?" None of the senior class knew whom he was talking to.

Ted said, "No, sir. I want to be a teacher."

He chuckled and said, "You taught us." More laughter. The meeting was over, we went back to our classes, and the military left.

The chief asked the principal, "May I talk to that young man?"

"Come back after school is out." The chief and the two men that went swimming were waiting for Ted.

"I gave you my decision earlier. No."

"Would you train us to fight like you did to me and Fred?"

"It is called martial arts. Karate. I am a third-degree black belt." A pause. "I don't know if I can help you and your team. School comes first, then Saturday, I am training some children." Nancee and Ted walked away. Back in school for the rest of their senior year and graduation. Nancee was helping Ted teaching the younger students learn how to defend themselves if approached by a stranger that wants to abduct you.

The class came to an end for the day. Ted and Nancee were worn out. The parents picked up their children. "Dad, I cannot take any more beating from those children." The four laughed. Ted was on his way to take Nancee home.

"I don't want to go home. Do we have enough money to rent a motel room?" Ted looked at her and smiled. He went to the motel office and rented room 8. He and Nancee walked into the room to find several Mexicans in the room. The illegals tried to stop Ted and Nancee. Instead, all the illegals were knocked out and lying on the floor.

Nancee went to the office and told the manager. He called the police. The manager, owner, didn't know that was happening. The police found a tunnel opening in the closet. Ted and Nancee got their money back and a clean room for the night. The tunnel was over six hundred yards long.

Sunday morning, Ted and Nancee walked out of the room very happy. The school year came to an end, and the whole class graduated. Ted and Nancee were married on July 4, 1965. Ted and Nancee found funds for college before school started. Nancee's parents saved enough money for her to attend all four years. Ted knew his funds were already set if he kept his grades up. Both of them finished college with a GPA of 3.86 each.

ONE LOST MAN

I met a man while on vacation. He asked, "Would you help me find my home? I don't know which way to go."

"Well, sir, what can you remember? Where have you been?"

"Well, young man, I think I was born. I didn't see any eggshells around me. It was colder than a well digger's foot, so maybe I was born in a cold state."

"That puts you in the north, but which state? All of them are cold during the winter. Do you remember a name of the state?"

"Well, I remember living in Walla Walla, Lewiston; Salem, Oregon; Charleston, South Carolina; and Charleston, Oregon. Waldport, Oregon; San Diego, San Francisco. Utah, Wyoming."

"Did you have any special friends when growing up?"

"Yes, I did, but they are all dead. I am the only one left in my family and our high school graduation."

"Wow. How old are you? Are you sure all your friends are gone?"

"Yes, I am sure. I think I just turned 105 years old."

"Don't you mean years young?"

"No, I mean old. I am not young anymore." He got tears in his eyes. "I am lost, and I don't know where to go."

"Have you been into any warmer states?"

"Yes, I think. I have been in Florida, Georgia, Texas, Missouri, and other southern states. I moved around so much I don't know where home is. Where do I call home?"

"Have you ever been married?"

"Yes. Six times. All of them died. I feel like Jerry Lee Lewis twice over."

"What is your favorite place to live?"

"I really don't know. I never spent much time in any one place. I did like North Carolina, but I don't like the eastern storms. Hurricanes are brutal. California has great weather, but it is hard to walk when the ground is shaking."

"What do you think about the central states, sir?"

"I can't swim anymore. Every spring, several states get flooded out due to the spring thaw."

"Pick a city you like. There must be some place you like."

"Not really. Most large cities are too dangerous to walk the streets any time of the day. Robbed, shot, and beaten up. For what? Being a human? I am too old to live in a large city."

"Then what about a small town? Do you think about some small towns that you lived in?"

"Yes. I like many of them, but my age keeps me from living there. Most of them don't have a doctor. Life is something that should have ended for me fifteen to twenty years ago."

"Do you have any friends to stay with? You must have someone to call. Do you remember any names?"

"All of them. Most of them died years ago." He started to cry again.

I stopped him from walking into heavy traffic. "You don't want to end your life that way."

"I get down when the weather gets cold and the rains start. Depression is very common for me." The man crossed the street with the walk light. "I never saw him again."

A young couple was sitting out on their front lawn in the shade of a large fir tree. This old man walked up the street and stopped to look at the house at 1818 Navajo Drive, Ogden, Utah. The wife asked, "May we help you, sir?" He didn't say a word, just stared at the house, turned, and walked on up the street.

In July 2087, an old man was found sleeping in a park close to a school in the city of Springfield, Missouri. An officer went to wake him and have him move on. He shook him twice then found out he was dead. An ambulance came and picked up the body. There was no identification on him. Two weeks had passed with no progress on identifying the old man.

The city put a picture of him in the paper. The picture went nationwide. Several thousand calls came in. A truck driver, Allen, said, "I gave him a ride to Boise, Idaho, from Ogden, Utah. He didn't talk much."

Another caller said, "My name is Michael. He was here in Raleigh, North Carolina, just a month ago. Didn't say much. He wanted some lunch money. I paid for his lunch and gave him twenty dollars."

The news came on at 5:00 p.m., Springfield, Missouri. "We have a great story for everyone to hear. Sit down and listen. Record this if you want. This will be two or three days long. We will start tonight at 8:00 p.m., so set your recorder."

At 8:00 p.m., the program started. "This story is about a Vietnam veteran SEAL team member. I know it sounds dull, but give us a try tonight. This man, James David Alberts, finished college at twenty-one years old. He has two degrees. One in electrical engineering. The second is mechanical engineering. The year was 1963. President Kennedy was shot and killed. Jim joined the Navy. He was officer material but turned it down. He said enlisted or nothing. He was in boot camp for two weeks, pulled out, and given the rate of petty officer second-class engineman."

A water break for John. Ted continued talking. "Jim wanted to be a SEAL. The training took several weeks, but he made it through. He was assigned to SEAL team 3 in San Diego. 1964 was his first trip to Vietnam. Several trips to home port and then back to Vietnam. He spoke the Vietnamese language very well, plus four other languages."

Another switch of commentators. "A bunch of officers were in a meeting with Jim and several other SEALs the summer of 1967. The American officers and SEALs were getting angry at the south Vietnamese army. Those men were not interested in fighting for their country. Many would cower off and hide when the close-to-base fighting started."

A break for that day. "Tomorrow, we will start at the same time. Tomorrow will not be as dull as today. Tomorrow, the crap hits the fan." Then he laughed.

Day 2 started with the TET offensive. David started talking. "The North celebrated their tenth anniversary of ousting the French from their country. All American bases were under attack from the NVA (North Vietnam Army). We were ready. The civilians warned us of the impending attacks on our bases. The South Vietnam Army were nowhere to be found."

John started talking. "After the battles were over, very few Americans were killed. Jim talked to the commander. He said, 'We are wasting our men for this garbage.' Those were not his exact words. I cannot repeat them on the air. Something like bull——."

Allen said, "Many officers and SEALs took a break from the fighting and flew to DC. President Johnson was in the war room. After kicking down the door, Jim stepped forward. "Mister President, This is a recording, so if you hear some bleeps, just put in your own word. Get your head out of your ——and end this stupid war. How much money are you making from your oil wells and your wife on her boat building?"

"No president has ever been beaten up by so many words than what Jim Alberts said to Johnson. His secret service escorted everyone out and said, 'Don't ever come back.'" A five-minute commercial break.

David started after the break. "The admiral of all the SEALs made contact with his troops. July 1968, 458 SEALs were flown to Vietnam. The Philippines was bypassed. All were onboard several LSTs and Destory Escort ships. At night time, some troops were loaded into ten-man rafts. Thirty rafts were in the water outside Haiphong Harbor. Their destination was Hanoi, the capital city. The rest of the SEALs and special forces went to Da Nang."

Another water break for listeners. John said, "Their north trip went fast. The SEALs managed to commandeer enough trucks for all the troops. Nighttime put them at the edge of the city. At the stroke of midnight, their actions were started. Haiphong Harbor lit up like a Fourth of July celebration. The troops moved into their designated areas. Jim, a lieutenant, and three more men went to the capital to visit Ho Chi Minh."

Allen continued. "Chief Petty Officer Jim Alberts put on his wicked fluorescent-lit Halloween mask of the devil with horns. Everyone walked into his bedroom. Jim leaned over the bed, shook the old man, and said in a deep voice, 'Ho Chi Minh, come with me.' He opened his eyes, looked at the devil, and had a heart attack. Dead on the spot. Most of his top officers were already killed in their beds."

Another break. Dave started. "Now with their travels southbound, their walk was to find and free all American prisoners. Several men were freed in Haiphong harbor and the Hanoi Hilton. The march south lasted seventy-three days. Every time some POWs were found, those men were trucked to the ocean and picked up by a small boat and taken to one of the hospital ships."

"President Johnson lost the presidency to president elect Nixon. The war was over. Hundreds of grave sites were found and marked with a gas-filled balloon. Helos would come in and dig up our soldiers and take them home in a body bag. The POWs freed was close to four thousand men. All the men on the walk received a silver star."

"Jim got out after eight years of service. He went home to Ogden where he met his wife, Samantha Cox, and her son, Michael, in 1975. Jim paid for her last year of college. She wanted to be a teacher but changed her mind. Jim let her go into the Navy as an officer."

The couple at the Ogden house looked at each other. Mike went up into the attic and brought down the box with the uniform and the devil's mask. "Mike said, "This is the mask that killed Ho Chi Minh." He didn't put in on, but got a picture of it. The next morning, Mike and his wife went to Hill Air Force base.

"We need to talk to your commanding officer. This box has the mask that killed the Vietnam dictator." The guard looked in the box and called the base CO. The CO was there in five minutes. He invited the young couple to his office. The General looked at everything in the box.

"I watched the story of Chief Alberts also. He did all those things and more. He received the Navy cross for gallantry. It wasn't until Congress went through some old records in 2002. Then he was presented with the Congressional Medal of Honor. He was sixty years old then. His wife retired from the Navy with twenty years of honorable service." Her uniform and medals were also in the box. "Thank you for keeping these uniforms and the medals. Janet, come in here. I want you to write up a pass for Mike and Sharon Kuffman to come shopping on base anytime. I will sign it."

"Thank you, sir. What will happen with this box of things now?"

"I will send everything to the Naval Museum in Norfolk, Virginia. He will find his place in history. Chief Alberts passed away in 2030 at eighty-eight years young. His wife, a retired Navy commander, died a month later. She could not live without Jim. She died from a broken heart. Their son, Michael, lost control of his senses. His mind snapped. No one saw him again."

"Sir, we know who that old man is. He is Michael Alberts. He stopped by several years ago, stopped, and stared at our, his, house and then walked on. We didn't realize that until this morning."

"I think you are right. I will call Springfield, Missouri, in a few minutes." He didn't have to. The doctors finally found his identity and put it out on the air. Michael was laid to rest by his parents. He died peace fully at the age of 114 years young. A few days later, after the museum set up the items of chief James Alberts, and his wife, a new female security guard, was walking past Chief Albert's display. The mask lit up. It scared her so much she ran away screaming while peeing in her pants. 'That mask is alive.'"

The display was covered at night and uncovered in the morning. A week later, the mask was gone from the display. There was a reward for the recovery of the mask. The cemetery for military personnel groundskeeper was cleaning up after another funeral. He walked past the Alberts' family plot. He stopped in surprise and saw the missing mask on Chief Albert's stone. It was embedded in his stone.

PHILLIP MICHAELS

Philip Michaels was born on March 11, 1935, in a small community of Mancos, Co. His father, Sam, and mother, Sally, had a small farm of ten acres about five miles from town. Dad was an electrical engineer working in Drango, thirty-one miles away. This property had been in the family for three generations, and they had no plans of selling.

Phil started the first grade in Mancos Elementary School. He was advanced to the second grade one week after starting school. His parents homeschooled him and his older brothers and sister before starting school. All their children skipped the first grade. The oldest, Sam Junior, skipped the third grade.

In 1941, now that Phillip was in school, Sally could go back to work. She worked in a grocery store in town just to have something to do. Phillip excelled through elementary and high school. He started his college at Pueblo Community College in 1953. Phil went to Durango, Co. to Fort Lewis College to finish his last two years. He graduated with an average grade of 3.88. His major was mechanical engineering, with a minor in business management. Back at home, he was in the house alone. His parents moved to Denver, Colorado. Sam got a better, higher-paying job a year earlier. Phillip put in his resume at the schools in town. "Would you please put me on your substitute teacher's list? I am not interested in moving right now."

Phil worked at a gas station to have some extra money. His dad set up an account for him until he could land a full-time job. In 1957, the school year started, but he continued working at the gas station. An old car limped into the station for fuel. There was a For Sale sign on the side window. A 1937 Lincoln Zephyr for sale, three hundred dollars. Phil's eyes lit up when he read the sign. He had more than enough to get the car, but he should call his dad first.

The family was in a hurry, so Phil thought, *Dad can yell at me later*. He asked them to wait a few minutes. He said, "I have the money in the bank across the street. Ten minutes, please." Phil told his boss what he wanted to do. "Does he have a clear title on that old car?" John went with Phil and asked to see the title. He brought out a good title in his name, Mike Johnson. His driver's license matched.

Mike signed the title over to Phil then asked, "Where is the bus depot?"

Phil said, "It is about one block down this street, with a restaurant next door."

Mike said, "Thank you." He got his belongings and family out and walked to the bus depot.

"The body is in good shape. The engine will need to be overhauled. I need to find a book to make the repairs properly," Phil said.

Phil dialed his parents' number.

"Hi, Mom, I love you."

"What did you do?"

"Is Dad still at work? I bought an old car. A 1937 Lincoln Zephyr four-door sedan."

"Does it run? Does it have the V12 engine?"

"Yes, Mom. The first is yes, but the V12 engine will have to be rebuilt." Phil finished the day and hooked up the Zephyr to a tow bar and towed it home. He parked it in the two-car garage. Phil went back into town, went to the bookstore, and asked for the automotive books. Carl took him to the right section, picked out the book, and handed it to Phil.

"How much is this book?"

Carl said, "Five dollars."

Phil paid him and said, "Thank you very much, Carl." His dad called shortly after he got home.

"Well son, how long will it take you to over haul the engine? You do know their gas milage is very low. About ten miles per gallon."

"No, I didn't know that, but I think I can find a way to increase the mileage on the engine."

"Where are you working? Did you get a teaching job yet?"

"Not yet, Dad. I am working at the gas station in town. It buys my food and pays the bills."

"Well, son, don't spend too much time on the car until you get a better job."

Phil said, "Thank you, Dad. I won't." He opened the garage door, only to watch it fall off its hinges. It missed the Zephyr by inches. Phil cussed a little then put the door back on its hinges, with some reinforcement. Phil started removing the grill so he could pull the engine. He stopped and removed the garage door, pulled the zephyr out, and towed it to the barn.

The next morning, Phil got a shower and then went to work. John said, "You need to go to the elementary school. Are you on the substitute teacher list?"

"Yes, I guess I better change." Three minutes later, Phillip was on his way to school. He arrived at school and walked in the principal's office, met with Mr. Paulson, and talked a couple of minutes. Mr. Paulson took Phillip to the seventh-grade classroom. Phillip introduced himself. "I am Mr. Michaels. I will be here until Mr. Jensen can come back to teach." From September 20 to November 24, Phil was happy to have a good job.

He was called to the principal's office. He walked in and asked, "Is Mr. Jensen back?"

"No." A long pause. "Mr. Jensen passed away a few minutes ago."

Phil sat down. "Oh my god, how will I tell the class?" He walked in and walked behind his desk. He stood up and erased Mr. Jensen's name, turned around, and said, "I am so sorry. Mr. Jensen passed away a few minutes ago." Two girls got up and walked next to Sally. She broke down and started crying. Phil didn't know what to do. The girls held her, trying to console her.

Garred said, "Mr. Jensen is her father."

"I am sorry, Sally, I did not know." He went to her, picked her up, and carried her to the principal's office. She would not let go of Phil's neck. Phil walked outside, holding Sally, and placed her in the back seat of her mom's car with her brothers.

Jeanie Jensen said, "Thank you, Mr. Michaels." She also had tears in her eyes but was still able to drive.

Phil went back to the classroom, to a lot of noise. The chatter stopped when he walked in the room. He said, "Don't stop, speak your mind." The talking went on for the rest of the day. The last bell rang, but the class was still talking.

Phil said, "Are you going home today? The buses are waiting for those that live out of town. Will you all be back tomorrow?"

Mr. Paulson came into the room and sat down. The two talked for an hour. He said, "The class really likes your way of teaching." The funeral was four days later. Most of the class and previous classes were at his funeral. Mr. Jensen's classmates also came. All the teachers showed up. Sally got up and pulled Phil over to sit by her family. She held his arm through the whole ceremony.

Phil got home, fixed some lunch, then went out to the barn, and finished pulling the engine out of the Lincoln Zephyr and put it in the back of his pickup. He moved the engine to the other part of the garage. Phillip drove to a metal shop in Durango. He talked to them about making a four-piece roll-up garage door. He drew up a plan for them to follow. Phillip had already written a patent and would submit it this next week. He said, "I would like the panels made from 16-gauge steel."

Eighteen days later, Phil received a call from the steel company. "Your door is ready. When can we install it?"

Phil said, "Anytime you want. I will be home all day on the weekends."

Jerry said, "We will see you Saturday, okay?"

"That sounds good to me. See you then."

Saturday came, and Phillip waited for his door to arrive. At twelve-thirty, the installers showed up.

Their boss said, "Please give us some time to figure out how to do this type of door. This is our first like this."

Phil said. "I will give you all the time you need."

The Steel Co. manufactured everything from scratch. The job took them four hours to complete.

John knocked on the front door. "Mr. Michaels, the door is done, I think." He chuckled. Phil went outside to look at the door.

"It looks good. Will the door roll up?" Mike went to the door and opened it. He turned the handle and lifted the door. It went up easily. The coil springs made the opening simple and feel light.

Phil asked, "Would you like to do one more?" pointing to the other garage door. The boss looked at his crew. Everyone said yes.

With all the forms made and material on hand, on Monday, the door panels were completed in seven hours; the hinges and track for one door was also ready the next day. There were two keys for each door. Jerry called Phil on Tuesday and said, "Everything is ready. When can we come out and install the second door?"

Phil said, "Tomorrow will be fine."

The next day, around 3:30 p.m., the door installation team started by removing the old door and set up the first panel. Some trimming had to be done first. The door and all parts were in place and working in about an hour.

Phil was called to test his new garage door. The door opened and closed with ease. Phil paid five hundred dollars for each door. Parts and labor were awfully cheap. The next week brought two men wanting to buy his patent. Before Phillip could say anything, three more cars showed up. All of them wanted the patent for their own company.

Phil said, "Get into your car. Write up your offer and give it to me. Don't try to be cheap. If you do, I will throw them away." Five minutes later, he was given all four offers. Phil went up on the porch, sat down, and looked through their offers. He motioned to them to come up and have a seat. "I will let each you have a copy of my patent for two million dollars each. That is less than any of your offers. Do you agree?"

The men looked at each other. One of them said, "How can you split a patent like that?"

"You are lawyers—you figure it out. If you don't agree, then get off my property." The men conversed for a few minutes. Phil went inside to get something to drink. He came out and sat in a chair on his porch. All of them walked up to the porch. One man brought up some forms for Phil to look at. The four companies agreed, so Phil signed the contracts, giving them each a copy of the patent. Phil received eight million dollars. He would keep the two garage doors. He gave each of them a copy of the blueprint and said, "Have a nice day."

Phillip Michaels made the check deposits into his bank account. Most of the money went to savings. Two million went to checking. IRS received their share. Phil still had over five million dollars. He went to Durango, Colorado, and visited the steel company. Jerry was excited about their new contract. "The local Sears store wants us to make garage doors for Colorado area and spread out to other states if possible."

Phil said, "That is great, then I guess you don't want these bonus checks for a job well done."

"I didn't say that. How much are they?"

"Not much, just thirty thousand dollars each. Can you handle that? If not, I will cancel them." Phil had a broad smile on his face. He handed Jerry the checks. "One each, and put your name on 'pay to the order of.'" They were really excited about the generosity of Mr. Michaels. Phil told them, "I sold the patent to a group of four companies. You earned these checks."

The secretaries stood there, looking disappointed.

"I didn't forget you, ladies. This is for you two. There is fifteen thousand dollars each." Sally opened the briefcase, dropped it on the table, cleared the table with one leap, wrapped her arms around Phil, and gave him a hug and several kisses while lying on the floor.

Her husband said, "She is very excitable." When the other woman came toward him, he put his guard up.

She, Tammy, said, "Thank you very much, sir." She gave him a hug and a long kiss.

Phil said, "You are very welcome."

Jerry said, "We were contemplating bankruptcy. The Sears contract and this money will keep us going for many years to come." Each of the employees gave Phil a handshake and a hug. Phil left the shop and headed home.

Phillip ordered the engine parts that he needed from the antique parts supply store. He spent three weeks putting the engine together then put it in the car. Phil answered the phone. His mom was on the other end.

"Don't you ever answer your phone?"

"I was busy, Mom, making some extra money. I want to go to Hawaii this summer, and I want you and Dad to go with me."

"Well thank you, son, but we cannot afford the trip."

"I am paying for it, Mom."

"Do you know how much that will cost?"

"I have plenty of money. Don't worry about the cost. I will come up there in a week or so, then we can talk about when we will go. Okay? I love you, Mom." Phil hung up and went to the garage and put the finishing work on the fuel conversion for the Zephyr. After a few test and adjustments, the engine was running well.

Phillip Michaels filed for a patent on his fuel economy project.

He loaded up some clothes and headed for Denver to spend some time with his family. He was driving the Lincoln Zephyr. Once he got on the inner state, he was cruising easily. A two-day trip. His parents greeted him with a hug and a kiss from Mom. His two brothers and older sister were there. Peggy was living at home after a nasty divorce. She kept custody of her daughter, two-year-old Molly.

Sam Junior and Gary were working for a lumber company. The wages weren't bad. Phil was the only one to go to college. Dad asked. "Did you change the engine? You know the stock V12 gets lousy gas mileage."

"I know that, Dad, but I can live with it. I averaged only eighty-four miles per gallon on the trip up here."

"Son, you are crazy. Let me see that engine." Phil opened the hood, and everyone was looking at it.

"That is a stock engine. What is that thing?" Sam Junior asked.

Phil said, "That thing is my latest patent. My first netted me five million, three hundred thousand dollars. Do you need some spending cash, Dad, Mom?" Neither one could say a word. Just stood there with an open mouth. He added, "When do you want to go for a flight to Hawaii? All of you."

A week later, they were in the air headed for Los Angeles. Phillip's car was locked up in Dad's garage. They landed in Los Angeles and then boarded a Hawaiian Airlines plane. Five hours in the air, and finally they landed at Honolulu International Airport. Their rooms were booked before they left Denver. The ride to the hotel was fast. They got checked in.

Mom said, "I would like something to eat. Where can we go?"

Down in the lobby, Dad asked the desk clerk for some good food. "We have a restaurant back there," he said, pointing toward the beach. Lunch was great. Everyone got filled up.

Phil asked Peggy, "Want to go for a walk? I want to see what is out there in this area." We all went together for a walk and sightseeing.

Mom bought a couple of souvenirs. Back at the hotel, they went out to the beach side and ordered some appetizers and some drinks. Peggy wanted to get a swimsuit for her and Molly. Phil gave her sixty dollars.

Dad asked, "Phil, what would you be asking for the fuel economizer?"

He said, "I am not sure, maybe one hundred million."

Gary said, "I was watching the news a while back. The oil companies have to disclose their quarterly earnings. The last report was an average of forty billion each for the top five oil companies."

A young woman came into the hotel lounge, reading a newspaper.

She heard Gary talking. "Excuse me, sir, here is the latest oil company earnings." She handed Phil the paper. They looked at it.

"I was close," Gary said.

She said, "My name is Phillis Morres. Do you work for one of the oil companies?"

Phil said, "No, we were just curious on how much money the oil companies make each year. I am a teacher. My name is Phillip."

He stood up and moved over to her table. Sam, Gary, and Dad headed for the beach where Mom and Peggy and Molly were. The two talked for over three hours. "Young lady, are you hungry? I am."

She said yes. Phil got up and took Phillis's hand. "Let's go find something to eat."

Phillis said, "There is a nice place across the street that I like." They went over there and ordered some good food. After eating, they went back to the hotel, then to the beach. They found a clear area and sat on the sand and continued talking.

They went to the bar and ordered a glass of bourbon on the rocks. Phil and Phillis then headed up to Phillip's room. The two talked more then made love.

Phillis started to cry. "Phillip, I don't have any right, but I want to get out of Hawaii. I do have a bachelor's degree in finance, but nobody wants to hire me here." She paused. "If you will help me get back to Boise, I can find a job there and pay you back, please?"

Phil held her for a minute. "You don't need to pay me anything, honey. When do you want to leave?"

"I can be ready in one hour."

"You can't go like that. You need some clothes on your beautiful body."

She smiled and held Phillip and said, "I need a shower." The two washed each other's back and butt and other parts. After drying off and getting dressed, Phillip followed Phillis to the place she was staying. Her friend was home. The girls talked while Phillis packed her suitcases. She said, "Thank you for putting up with me. My friend is helping me get home to Idaho. I will be able to find a good job there, and I can send you some money to pay you back."

Marji said, "Well, if you are leaving, I am going back home also. The manager raised my rent this month. My home is in Las Vegas. With my bachelor's degree in finance, I might be able to get a job with one of the mob bosses." They all laughed.

"Marji, do you have enough money to get back home?"

"I think so. I will sell some of my things to give me the extra cash I will need." Phil brought out his wallet. Marji said, "No, I don't want it."

Phillis said, "Don't look at me. I am not his boss."

Marji said, "How much will I need? I have saved two hundred thirty dollars."

"Phillis, honey, how much is your ticket to Los Angeles?

"One hundred forty-two dollars."

Marji went next door and asked Karen if she still wanted the things she had.

She said, "I am going home today." She was almost crying. "These are happy tears."

Karen said, "I have looked at what you had before." She came over to Marji's apartment and looked at everything. "Will three hundred dollars be enough?"

Marji held Karen and said, "Thank you." Phillip helped move everything Karen wanted. That included the bedsheets and pillows. The living room and kitchen items were all gone and moved to Karen's apartment. Marji had all her things packed, and Phillip rode to the airport with them.

The ladies bought their tickets to Los Angeles, and there, the two would go different ways but never forget each other. The two had gone through four years of college together. Marji had a decent job but had to scrape to save what she did manage to save. Both women gave Phillip a hug and kiss and asked, "Will we ever see you again?"

"Of course. Here is my phone number. Please don't lose it, baby." Another kiss and hug. Phil gave Phillis an extra five hundred dollars. "Time to go, your plane is loading." Phil went in the dining room and sat down with the family.

"Where did you go? We lost track of you."

"Phillis went home to Idaho. I met her girlfriend. She is beautiful also."

Gary asked, "Where is she? I would like to meet her. I am a decent person, aren't I?" Dad laughed.

Phil said, "She has a master's degree in psychology."

Gary asked, "What is that?"

Dad broke out in laughter. "She is a head shrink."

They placed their order and talked for a while before their food came.

Mom asked, "Did Phillis go to college?"

"Yes, she did. I saw her bachelor's degree. She and Marji went to school together. Both of them have a degree in finance. The two are on their way to Los Angeles. Marji lives in Las Vegas. Phillis lives in Boise."

Their food came, and they were mostly quiet while eating. They already made plans to leave in two days. Phillip wanted to get back home and try to find a Lincoln Zephyr two-door coup. Phil had heard that there were a couple of places in Wyoming that had many old cars.

They made our flight to Los Angeles and then to Denver. "Dad, are you interested in getting an old car or truck and restoring it?"

"I have thought about it, but I haven't ever had enough money, and now I am too old to do the work."

"You are not too old, Dad, and you have the money. I am giving you and Mom half a million dollars. Don't tell me no! Okay?"

"Where would I find a vehicle from the thirties and forties?"

Gary said, "I heard about a place in Wyoming a couple hundred miles west of Cheyenne on Highway 225. When do you want to check them out?"

"Give me a couple days to rest from all the excitement we had in Hawaii." dad said.

Mom said, "You are not going anywhere without me. I would like a small coup. Ford, Chevy, I am not particular."

Gary asked, "Will we be on your list of some money to help our financial problems?"

Phil rubbed his ears. "I think I heard some buzzing in my ears." Then he laughed. "Yes, Gary, you and your brother. I would like Peggy and Molly to come home with me for a while."

Dad said, "We can go and look at the vehicles tomorrow. Sam and Gary, will you two bring your trucks?"

Phil said, "I guess I should have brought my truck."

Sam Junior said, "I will call Fred and maybe we can use his help. He has a HD Ford and a double trailer. It will hold two cars."

The next morning, Fred showed up with his truck and trailer.

Gary said, "With three pick-ups and Fred's truck, we will be able to bring back a bunch of toys." They headed up to 225 and turned west. Fred knew where the antique auto yard was. He had been there before. Phil drew out fifty thousand dollars. Fred called, and the owner opened the gates. They found that Fred was related to the owner, Mike.

Mike greeted us. "Welcome to the yard. Fred is my cousin. I would not have let you in. You are total strangers to me." Fred closed the gate.

Phil said, "Thank you, Mike and Fred. I am looking for a Lincoln Zephyr coup. '36 or '37. My mom—"

Mike said, "I will show you what I have, and Fred, show the Mrs. where her choice of cars are."

Phil and Mike walked to where the Lincolns are. Phil look at all he had. He had two Zephyr coups. A '36 and a '41.

"How much do you want for the '36 coup?"

"Three thousand dollars." Phil said okay.

"You are not going to barter?"

"I don't want to get us kicked out with nothing."

"Okay, two thousand dollars. I will get my truck and take it up front. wait here." Mike brought his special truck for moving cars and trucks. Mom found her '35 Ford three window coup. It was still in decent condition. Fred moved it up front. Next, Dad picked out a '39 Ford pickup. Mike moved it up front, and went back to get Sam's '39 Ford pickup. Gary decided on the '37 Ford pickup.

Mike asked, "Are you through shopping?" Dad looked at us and said yes.

"How much do you owe us?" then laughed. Mike also laughed. Mike added up the prices and said "Nine thousand three hundred dollars." Phil went over to dad's truck and pulled out his briefcase, opened it, and brought out ten thousand dollars. The money was in packs of five thousand dollars.

Mike said, "This is ten grand."

"I know, I don't want to break the bundle. Give some to Fred for the use of his truck and trailer."

"Fred, can you get the coups on your trailer?" He said yes.

Mike and Fred got the coups loaded on Fred's trailer, while Dad and the boys put the pickups on their tow-dollies. They all thanked Mike and Fred for helping them. Mike gave Fred three grand. He said, "Thank you, Mike." After three hours and thirty minutes, they were home. They all helped Fred get the coups off his trailer.

"Thank you again, Fred," Phillip said. Everyone thanked Fred. They moved Mom's coup and Dad's pickup out back, then the boys went home with their trucks.

The next morning, Dad and Phil put the Lincoln Zephyr coup on a tow dolly. Phil said, "Dad, my car will tow the coup." The dolly was still on his truck. He thought for a little bit. "How much cash do you have?"

"I will check." Phil checked and said, "Sixty thousand."

"Can I borrow off the other money? I want a newer truck. I have a friend that wants this one."

"I will take you to the bank and make the transfer, okay?" Dad said okay. Mom went with them. They were in the bank thirty minutes. The money was transferred to their account. Dad withdrew ten thousand. Phillip went out to the parking lot.

Dad looked at the Dodge Pickups. Mom rode with Dad in a very comfortable riding pickup. Mom said, "This is so much better than your Ford truck. Do you like this color?"

"Yes. How much do you want for this pickup?"

The dealer said, "Nine thousand four hundred and eighty-eight dollars."

They headed home with Dad driving a new truck. Mom was also very happy. Phil helped put the old pickup and coup up out of sight. We left the next morning. Peggy and her daughter, Molly, rode with Phil. They drove for four hours before we stopped for a break. They rested for a half hour.

Dad said, "We will stop for the night in Pueblo. There is a nice motel in town on the east side. Save us a room."

"Mom, you are acting sore. Switch with Peggy. This is more comfortable than that truck." Dad was driving.

"Peggy can drive for a while." Mom rode with Phil for the rest of the trip to Pueblo. They were there about an hour before Dad and Peggy. Mom and Phil rented three rooms. Phil went to the office and used his phone in the lobby. The phone rang three times before someone picked it up. The voice said hello. Phil said, "Hi, is Phillis there?"

"Who is this?"

"I am Phillip. I met her in Hawaii."

"Hello," came from the phone.

"Hi, honey, how are you doing?"

She almost started crying. "I love you, baby. Can I come down there with you? My family didn't want me to come back."

"I am on my way back home now." She started crying.

"Do you have any of the money I gave you left?"

"No. It went real fast. My dad has not worked for a while. He broke a leg. The medical bill is high."

"When I get home, I will come up there and get you. Okay, baby? I love you, honey. My dad just got here. I will be home tomorrow. Love you. Please be patient, honey. Go out and call collect tomorrow after noon. Bye, sweetheart."

"I love you." She hung up.

Phil called Phillis's mom and asked for Phillis. We talked for a few minutes.

He said, "Go to the Western Union and pick up some money. Three hundred fifty dollars, and take your baggage with you. Then go to the airport hotel and get a room for the night. Your flight will be leaving at 9:35 a.m." He gave her the PSA flight #. "Did you get all that written down?"

She said, "Western Union, pick up money, then go to the airport hotel. Sleep good tonight, and catch PSA flight number at 9:35 to where?"

"Denver, Colorado. With adjoining flight to Durango, Colorado."

"You will arrive in Durango about 1:25 p.m. I will be waiting for you, sweetheart. I love you."

"I love you too."

"On more thing is the Western Union password, PPS. Write it down."

"I got it. I love you, honey." She hung up and packed her bags. Her mom drove her to Western Union and to the airport hotel. She gave her mom a hug and two hundred dollars. "I love you mom. I just wish things were a lot better than what you, Dad, and the children are having to deal with. I am going to find a job and send you some money each month. Okay, Mom?"

"She said, 'I love you too, baby.' Take care of yourself. I am also sorry things didn't work out here."

Phillis got out and took her baggage to the hotel. Phillis was up early, checked out, and rode the hotel bus to the airport. Phillis checked her luggage then found something for breakfast. She checked the time and headed for the boarding area. The plane landed in Denver. She left that plane and headed for the loading area to fly to Durango. Phillis walked to the loading area. Phillip and his parents were waiting for their flight back to Denver. Phil said, "I left my briefcase in your house. Let my brothers share the money. There is sixty thousand dollars in it. I will set up an account for Peggy so she will have some money. She has mentioned that she wants to finish her college. Peggy said she would like to teach."

"Time to go, the plane will be landing soon," Dad said.

The plane landed. Phil and his parents were waiting. Phillis walked off the plane and ran over to Phillip. She was so excited she started crying while holding Phillip tight. Phillis finally released Phil and said, "I am so happy, sweetie. Please don't ever leave me." She started crying again.

Phil said, "I don't plan on letting you get away, honey. When I saw you, I said to myself, 'She is the one I have been looking for.' I fell in love with you when I first saw you."

We said goodbye to Mom and Dad. Phil put Phillis's bags in the back seat of the 1937 Lincoln Zephyr. Phil opened the passenger door. Phillis got in and sat down. Phil got in the driver's seat. He drove to his house then helped her out and got her baggage. He carried them up, and Peggy opened the door. "Hi, Phillis. I am Peggy, the third of the family."

Phillis said, "I remember you. I thought you two were married, and my heart fell to the bottom of my stomach. Then you introduced me to your family. My heart started beating again." She gave Peggy a hug.

Peggy said, "I will not be here long. I will be going back to school to finish my degree to become a teacher. I completed one year then Molly came along. I think I will go to Durango to Fort Lewis College." Peggy dug through her luggage and found her credits for her first year.

She came into the kitchen and fixed breakfast for Molly and herself. "I will take Molly with me. I have my fingers crossed."

Phillis said. "You will always have a room here."

Peggy was coming home. She was happy. "Must be good news," he said.

Peggy said, "Yes, I spent the day testing. What do you want for supper?" Molly was watching cartoons. Phil said, "We need another TV."

Peggy said, "Molly."

Phil said, "That's fine—the news isn't on yet."

Supper was ready, so they all sat down and ate.

"Well sis, how was your trip to the college?"

"Great. I was tested on many subjects to find out if I am ready to continue with my second year. It has been three years since I left school. I amazed myself. My average grade was just 3.7. I will start my second year this fall. I am really excited. I have been assigned a room at the campus housing. Molly can stay with me. The college has a day care for single and married women." She was so happy she had tears in her eyes. "Mama don't cry."

"Honey, these are happy tears."

"I will set up an account for you to cover school supplies, food, and rent. Is there anything else you need?"

"Clothes, Molly is growing. She has grown one inch this summer."

"Will twenty-five thousand dollars be enough?" Phil said.

Peggy jumped up and wrapped her arms around Phil. "Thank you, brother. You are the greatest brother in the world." Peggy moved to the dorm at Fort Lewis College the next day. School started for Phillip. He was back teaching the seventh grade. Earlier, Phillip spent over four thousand dollars on supplies for the school. Crayons, pencils, all the basic stuff, and backpacks plus dictionaries for every class from fourth grade to the senior high school class.

Peggy was off for Thanksgiving. The elementary school was having a special play on the weekend. Phil and Peggy knew what was planned. Some of the teachers knew but kept quiet. Phillip and Phillis were there in the front row. The program went well, then Phillip was asked to come up and say something. "Honey, come up with me." She said no, but Phil talked her in to getting up on the stage with him.

He said a couple of things and looked at his shoes. In the middle of his talk, he knelt down, reached in his jacket pocket, and pulled out a little box. Phillis got instant tears in her eyes. Phillip opened the box and said, "Phillis Morres, will you marry me?" She did not hesitate.

"Yes." He stood up and placed the ring on her finger and gave her a kiss.

December 30, 1963, the couple was married. Phill gave Phillis a check for her family. He said, "Write a note to your parents, and mail this to them." Her father's name, John Morres, was on the check.

Phillis said, "Thank you, honey, the whole family will benefit from this." The check was for two hundred fifty thousand dollars.

After school started in January, Phillip was back teaching. Part of the weekend was set aside to work on the 1936 Lincoln Zephyr coup. The coup was ready for a test drive on August 5, 1965. Over a year of work, Phillip and Phillis went for a ride. The coup was just as fast as the sedan. The 1937 sedan had light blue paint. The coup had medium light gray paint. Phillis learned how to drive a stick shift. She really loved the '36. That was her favorite car. The 1957 Chevy was feeling lonely. Phillip drove the Chevy to school for a week, then the 1937 zephyr sedan would be parked in his school parking spot.

Phillis was ready to deliver her first child. She had twins packed in her belly. They received a call from her mother. She wanted to come down to our house.

Phillis asked, "What took you so long to call? Yes, Mom, fly to Denver then transfer to Durango. Call before you leave Denver so we can be in Durango to pick you up."

"Thank you, honey. My flight will put me down in Durango at one thirty p.m."

"What day, Mom?"

"Today, is that too soon?"

Phillis laughed. "Oh, Mom, no, we will be there to pick you up."

Phillis was due any day now. They drove to the Durango airport and waited for the plane to land. Janet saw them, came over, and gave Phillis a hug and kiss.

"We were so happy to see that check. Thank you, Mr. Michaels."

She hugged him and said, "We are doing much better now. Dad is back working at a different auto repair shop. Dad is the foreman now." They put her suitcase in the back seat then started to leave.

Phillis let out a yell. "Take me to the hospital—it is time." Phillip headed for the hospital. They got there, and Phillis went to check in. Her mother went with her. Phil parked the Chevy and ran into the hospital, went to the delivery room, and had to wait. After forty-five minutes, she went back to the delivery room. The first baby was our very beautiful daughter, and after a couple minutes more, the second baby was out. A very handsome boy. Our choices of names were Samantha and Sam.

Two days later, Phil and Janet went to the hospital and picked up the twins and Phillis and headed home. They were all happy. Janet called home and gave everyone the news. "Honey, you have two grandchildren."

ROBERT AND PEGGY

Robert Vick was working for General Electric in California. He made several items for home. A generator for bad weather. When an item goes up for sale, the inventor gets 25 percent of the earnings. His annual pay was forty-five thousand dollars in 1985. Now he was making more income with the generator. Rob was working on another design. This will go for trailers and fifth wheels and RVs.

The design was only five horsepower. It would run off a battery and recharge the battery at the same time. This item went on the market. GE could not keep up with the request for it. Rob was now making sixty-four thousand dollars each year. With his two inventions, his monthly income was another seven thousand dollars. The truck drivers also wanted one for their long-haul trips. The heater driven generators were a lifesaver for them during the cold winter snow trips.

Six years working for GE, he was working on a special project. It was being built in his garage. He had saved most of his money and started a fidelity account. It just went over four million dollars. Four more years passed. He turned in his resignation to GE after ten years. He was now on his own. Six months had passed. He was still getting money for the other items he made with GE. Six months after leaving GE, his money stopped coming in.

He wasn't worried because he had just finished his project. He took it to the small planes airport in east San Jose. The truck scared him. The speed went up to 115 mph in less than a mile. His truck was an electric-powered vehicle. The small gas engine was the starter. It turned the generators and motor. The generators took over then. He had a five-speed transmission to move the truck. Rob drove the truck to Detroit and called the three auto giants together.

After a test run each, the CEOs talked and started making offers. Rob stopped them and said, "I will accept twenty-five million each."

The three companies said, "Fifteen million each."

Rob accepted their offer. "I am not that greedy." He rode a bus and headed home to Missouri where his parents and siblings were living. At the bus depot, he called home and asked for a ride. "I am at the bus depot in Springfield." His younger sister picked him up.

Shelly said, "What are you doing here? Where is your truck?"

"I left it in San Jose. I just came from Detroit."

"What were you doing up there?"

"A business trip. I don't work for GE anymore." His parents heard part of the conversation.

"Son, why did you quit? Now what are you going to do?"

"Retire. I have saved enough to stop working."

Mom said, "What are you hiding, son? You are only thirty-one."

He talked about his projects built while working for GE. "I quit working for them and went out on my own. My last project I just sold it to the three auto manufacturing companies for forty-five million dollars." Dad and Mom fell down on their couch. Shelly couldn't say anything. Just stood there with an open mouth.

"I am moving out of California. I hate the shaking every other day. I am thinking about Utah. First, I will put my house up for sale and look for a place in northern Utah. I want to learn how to snow ski." A pause. "Mom, Dad, are you ready to retire?"

Dad said. "Not yet, son. Give me another twenty years."

"I want to transfer five million to each of you to a fidelity account. Just one million to each of the children as they are born. Shelly, you will get two million dollars when you graduate."

Mom said, "No, honey. We will give her that much from our money." He said okay.

Shelly said, "Can I have ten children?" then she laughed.

Dad said, "Get married first, then you can have as many children as you want."

"Where is my Navy sister? Does she ever come home?" The doorbell rang. Shelly opened the door and wrapped her arms around big sis.

Sherri walked in. "My ears are ringing. Who has been talking about me?" We got up and gave her a hug. "I have two weeks off. Is it fishing season yet?"

Rob said, "I was talking about you. Can't you come home more often, sis? We all miss your company. I have some money for you." He set down and wrote her a check for two million dollars.

Sherri looked at it, fell down on the couch, and looked at Rob with a smile on her face. "What bank did you rob?"

"I sold my last patent for a bunch of money."

"I guess so. What am I going to do with this much money? I just made chief and reenlisted. The initiation will take place when I get back. I like the Navy. I will retire from the Navy. Just twelve more years."

"Start a fidelity account." We went fishing three different days.

Sherri said, "I have to go back to work now. Rob, are you still working for GE?"

"No, I quit last year to work on my last project. You will see it sometime this year hopefully." Dad drove Sherri and Robert to the airport. Sherri went to San Diego. Robert went to San Jose, put his house up for sale, and drove up to Ogden, Utah. He went through Nevada and stopped at all the big casino stops. He spent three thousand dollars and won two thousand dollars.

Now in Utah, he drove up to Ogden and went looking for a house. Robert rented an apartment. In 1998, he looked at a thousand houses. He went through Shadow Valley housing. "Wow, these places are for rich people." Then he laughed. He drove through every street, but no one wanted to sell.

One more street to check. From the west end to the east, stopped, and got out. A For Sale sign was in the yard. Rob walked up to the door and knocked. The man opened the door.

Rob said, "I will take it. How much do you want?" Rob and the man laughed.

"Come in. We are cleaning up the last room." He went back downstairs. "Look around. Three bedrooms down here and three upstairs." Rob went through the house, went out back and then back in. The couple were in the kitchen, waiting for Rob to come in.

"How much do you want? What is your asking price?"

"One hundred fifty-five thousand dollars."

"That sounds fair to me. Cash or check. Who is the realtor?"

"We are selling by owner. I will do the paperwork. Give me two days, okay?"

"I will be back with the money." Two days passed, and Robert showed up, looked over the papers, and both men signed. His wife also signed where required.

The man said, "The house is now yours." Robert handed him a check for one hundred fifty-five thousand dollars.

"Is this real?"

Rob said, "Yes, it is. Every penny of it. Check with the US bank."

He went to the bank. "Is this check good? Can I deposit it into my account without it bouncing?" The cashier looked at Rob's account.

"It is a good check, sir." She called Rob to verify the amount.

Rob said, "Yes, I did write it. I just bought his house." He came back and handed Rob the keys and garage door opener. Rob turned in the papers and insured the house through Alstate Insurance. He took a break and went to a bar downtown. He walked in and sat at the bar. The waitress was serving table customers. One man grabbed her arm.

"Sit with me because I like you." She tried to go to another table. He caused her to spill two glasses of beer on his lap. He pushed her and said, "Now look at what you did." He pushed her again. Rob stood up and hit him, knocking him down. He jumped up, and Rob hit him again. His friend stood up and got between Rob and his friend, who was still on the floor.

The big man was helped out and into their truck. The smaller man drove off and headed up the road. The woman had beer on her also.

The owner said, "I do not want them in here anymore. Peggy, go home. See you tomorrow." The owner got Rob a beer. "This is on me. What the hell did you hit him with?"

"My right hand." Peggy went home and was back in twenty minutes.

She came to Rob and set down with him. The two talked for several minutes. She whispered, "Will you take me home? I need someone to talk to. I am lonely." Rob stood up and took her hand, and the two walked out. Rob opened the passenger door, Peggy got in, and he closed the door and walked around, and got in. He drove to his apartment and opened the door.

She followed Robert to his apartment. She held him after getting into the room. "I hate that bar. That was not the first time he grabbed me. Thank you for knocking him out."

"The owner banned those two from his bar."

"That won't stop them. He will trash the bar just to be an ass that he is."

"Find another job. What can you do?"

She got tears in her eyes. "Nothing. I left home after graduating. My grades were 3.2. That is how dumb I am."

"Can you cook? I am tired of eating burnt food." Peggy laughed. Somehow she knew Rob was joking.

"Not all dumbs are blonde. I am proof of that."

"I will help you find a better job that pays a lot more than a bar. I'm hungry. What do you want to eat?"

"I like Wendy's. Is that all right?" The two got into his truck and headed to Wendy's. He turned off the main road and headed up to a lot.

"That is their truck. The man I knocked out."

Peggy said, "That is the police impound." She smiled. "Those two are in jail now."

"Drunk driving? Keep them in there for a long time." Rob went on to Wendy's, and the two had their supper. Back in his apartment, Robert and Peggy made love and then went to sleep. Peggy and Robert were very happy. Morning came, and Rob talked about Peggy taking classes for a tech school.

"I don't know what I can do. We will get a list of subjects from Weber State and you can look through the list to find something you feel will be easy for you."

"Honey, what did you do? Did you finish college?"

"Yes, I did. I am an electrical engineer. I was the first in my family to go to college."

"Do you really think I can get a decent job?"

"Everybody can. Their willpower and drive will get them a better job. I studied hard and came out with my degree. I can help you with your homework. I will not do your work, just help teach you how to study." She gave him a kiss. "I love you, honey."

"I love you too." Rob got a list of tech schools and gave it to Peggy. She looked through the list. "I don't know, honey. I am lost on what to select."

"Okay. Put the list aside for now. Just think about what you would like to be someday."

"I would like to be a wife and mother. I am twenty-nine now. Can I go back to the bar, honey?"

"Yes, you can. Be careful, sweetheart. I love you. I have to go to work also." Rob had his kitchen plan and went to Ikea to pick up his order. He hooked up his trailer and drove to the store. After getting everything loaded, he headed back to his house. He already had the kitchen ceiling vaulted. A contractor did it for him. Those two men also removed the old cabinets out of the kitchen.

Robert drove his truck up to the back porch and unloaded all the boxes. He stacked them in the living room and dining room areas. One at a time, the packages were opened, and he put the cabinet together. Twenty-six separate cabinets, thirteen on the top and nine on the bottom. Four for the island. The top was put up first. Six days to get the top done. Another four days for the bottom. Rob called the contractors again.

Robert said, "I need a counter top and back splash. Also a countertop for the island." He smiled. "Don't drink all my beer." The men laughed. He showed them what and how he wanted the counter top and back splash, then he walked out. One week had passed, and he looked at a beautiful kitchen.

"Do you know how to build a gazebo? The hot tub will be here in the morning." The hot tub was set in place. Rob wired it up while the contractors built the gazebo. Robert spent many nights with Peggy in his apartment while all the work was going on in his house. Time to get into his new home.

The contractor rented a back hoe to level out the garden, and then Rob would set up the rock wall with the help of the contractors. He was keeping them busy. The two men were loving it. He had paid them three thousand dollars each so far this month. The two men were also working on building a house. His jobs for them were weekends and days off.

Robert invited the two men to the bar for a few drinks. Neither one could make it. Rob showed up at the bar early. Peggy almost ran to him. He went down on one knee. She stopped and looked at him. He opened the ring box and asked, "Peggy, honey, will you marry me?"

Her eyes watered up with a yes! He placed the ring on her ring finger and got several kisses. All the regular customers applauded. We sat for a drink then left and spent their night in the apartment. The house was ready. We set a date for our wedding.

She called her parents. She started crying. "My parents can't make the trip."

"How far away are your parents?"

"Sacramento. Dad is not working now. His job ended because the company went out of business."

Rob called them. "Please, Mr. and Mrs. Franklyn, your daughter needs you here. I will get you two and your children a plane ticket to Salt Lake Airport. How many tickets do you need?"

"We will need five tickets."

"When can you be ready? Tomorrow? Don't worry about the cost. Okay?" Her dad said okay. Ten minutes later, Robert booked their flight. Peggy called and gave her parents the airlines, flight number, and time. Their flight would leave at 11:30 a.m. "Love you, Mom and Dad." She started crying. Rob held her. "Thank you, sweetie."

"My parents are coming from Missouri. I have to go to the airport to pick them up. You coming with me?" He was still in the apartment. He decided to stay there for another month. Each of his new house bedrooms had a bed in it, plus an extra bed by the downstairs fireplace. Each bedroom had a TV. Rob had new cables run for all the bedrooms and computer room.

He picked up his parents and little sister. Mom was expecting another baby son within a month. He took them to his new house.

"Pick a room, Mom, Dad. Peggy, I will stay in my apartment."

Peggy asked, "Oh my god, how long have you had this house? It is beautiful."

"Almost a year, honey. You will stay here with your parents downstairs, and I will be in the apartment for a few days." Dad took Peggy to the airport and picked up her parents and siblings. Rob's dad, Fred, brought them to their motel rooms. The mothers and Peggy went shopping for a wedding dress. "Rob didn't give me any money for a dress."

Rob's mom, Sharon, said, "I have the money, so don't worry about the cost." The hunt went for two days before a dress was found all three agreed on. Fred and Mark took Robert for a tuxedo hunt and suits for them. Fred paid for everything. Four days passed, and the day was here. Everyone went to the church. Robert was already there.

The wedding ceremony took twenty-five minutes, then everyone went to the new house for the reception. Mark and Patty were amazed at the size of the house.

Rob said, "It is only eighteen hundred square feet. I didn't get you a trip back to Sacramento. I will help you find a job here if you want to."

Mark said, "I have an offer in Sacramento when we get back."

"That is okay with us. We will visit quite often, Mr. Franklyn. This will keep your family going until you can find a job." Robert handed him a check for one hundred thousand dollars. He just stared at it. Fred took them to the airport and bought their plane tickets home.

"Our son likes spending money for friends and family. He has several million dollars to work on." Peggy and Robert said goodbye to her parents, brothers, and sister.

Fred and Sharon and little sister left for Missouri the next day.

ROBERTO GARCIA

Roberto was born in Magdalena de Kino, Mexico. He graduated from high school in June 2014 and started looking for work. Not many jobs were available in the small towns. He walked and hitch hiked to Nogales, Arizona. No passport or birth certificate to identify himself. He asked for a working visa. "You need some identification," the guard said.

Roberto went home and picked up his birth certificate. He had to work to get some money then went north again. Roberto was sent away once more. He went east and met many people. Some were willing to help him. Others were drug dealers, wanting him to take drugs across the border. He turned them down. Roberto got the crap beat out of him and left him for dead.

A passing farmer found him and took him home. His wife and a doctor nursed him back to a healthy condition. Roberto stayed and worked for the farmer and family for almost two years. He was paid a small wage. The farmer was not a rich person.

Roberto Garcia left with almost one hundred dollars in American money value. He headed on his easterly direction. Walked for a while, caught a ride for a while, then more walking. He made his way to Ciudad Juarez, Mexico. He was now nineteen. He walked on the pedestrian bridge most of the way to the border checkpoint. There he stopped and almost turned around. He took a deep breath, then continued to the El Paso, Texas, CBP checkpoint.

"I am Roberto Garcia, and I would like to work in the USA. All I have is my birth certificate. I am hungry." His eyes got watery.

There were two CBP agents there. One agent said, "Come with me, young man. I am Jose Rodriguez. I will help you the best I can."

"Thank you, sir. I don't have any formal training, but I can learn fast." He followed Mr. Rodriguez to the process office and sat while many papers were filed out. He had his fingerprints and picture taken. Signed a bunch of papers, received a working visa and a passport. He was crying now with happy tears in his eyes. He stood up and gave Mr. Rodriguez a hug.

"You will be staying at my house until you can find a job and a home of your own." Roberto met Jose's family. Their oldest was on his way to college, so Roberto's room was the vacant bedroom. Jose's wife, Laretta, washed his clothes. He was given some clothes to wear to add to his shortage of clothes. Jose had Roberto visited several shops over the next month.

After going to a welding shop, a machine shop, and a catering business, he took the body shop job. The body shop was not too far away. He was use to walking, so that didn't bother him. He showed up at the shop every morning on time. Many times before the shop was open.

He was getting minimum wages, but he didn't care. He had a job.

One year there and he received a pay raise. Roberto learned almost every aspect of repairing a vehicle. The crew liked him. He learned very fast and retained what he learned. At the same time, the crew taught him English. He was getting most of the words correctly in a sentence. Roberto now had a bank account of over four thousand American dollars. He had his own apartment next door to the body shop. Nine months now in his apartment and was very happy for everything the people did for him. He had no reason to go back into Mexico, but he wanted to retaliate against the bunch of drug dealers that almost killed him. He thought about it almost every day. Fourteen months without taking any time off, he asked, "Can I get a few days off and go home to visit my family?"

The boss said, "When do you want to leave, Roberto?"

"I would like to go on Monday for a week anyway. Will I have a job when I get back?"

The crew together said, "Yes, Rob. We will be waiting for your return. Be careful, please."

Roberto packed some clothes in a suitcase and left Monday morning on a bus to Nogales, Arizona. He was very excited. He has been away from home for three and a half years now. He had his working visa and passport with him everywhere he went. He got a ride to his hometown. Roberto walked to his parents' house and knocked on the door. Little sister opened the door. She screamed and jumped into his arms.

The rest of the family came running to see Roberto holding his baby sister. She was crying and not letting go. Mom and the rest of the family gathered around Roberto with wet eyes holding on to him. His father was still working. He won't be home for two hours or more. Roberto walked to the store with the family. He brought three thousand dollars with him.

The shopping lasted forty-three minutes. The whole family was very thin except for Roberto. The kids spent one hundred dollars, and Mom spent two hundred dollars more. Most all of the purchases were food. A few treats and some ice cream. Their dad heard that Roberto was home, so he left work early to spend time with the oldest child of the family. Dad was so happy he started crying along with Roberto.

Roberto was home for three weeks. He gave his mom and dad two thousand American dollars. "I am working in an auto body shop in El Paso, Texas. A CBP agent took me in and gave me a place to stay until I could afford my own place." The family asked a thousand questions and were happy to have him home for a while. Roberto had an exercise gym to work out in whenever he wanted to. He built up some bigger arms and chest. He was six feet, one inch tall. Dad was five feet, eleven inches tall.

"I have to go back to work in the morning, Dad, Mom. I have missed all of you." He held them all with a hug and said, "I will be back again next year. I promise, and I will bring some more money. My wages are real good." The morning came, and the family went with him to the bus depot. Dad went to work, and his mom and siblings walked back home. Roberto bought a bus ticket that took him through Mexico to the family that saved his life. He stopped the bus and got off. He was two miles from the town. He walked up to the door and knocked. The father answered the door.

Carlos recognized him and shook his hand. "I stopped to say hi and thank you for your help." He handed Carlos seven hundred dollars. "This is for saving my life, sir, ma'am. I have a job in El Paso, so I have to be leaving now. Thank you again for your help."

Roberto walked toward the town. He saw the boys that tried to kill him, so he walked up to their house, kicked in the door, and rushed in. He knocked three out real fast. The others ran at him. He hit one with a chair and busted the others mouth with his right foot, knocking him out. All five were out on the floor. He tied them up, gagged, and blindfolded them. The bunch of drug dealers were hog tied.

Roberto went through the house and looked for their drugs. He wanted to destroy all of it. In the process, he found their cash of money. He looked around and put the money—all of it was American money—into a large bag. He picked up his suitcase and the bag and left. He arrived at the bus station and got a ticket to the bridge to El Paso. He arrived there just before dark. Roberto walked up to the CBP checkpoint and identified himself. The agent asked, "Any drugs, weapons?"

He said, "No, sir. Just some money I found along the way here." He was smiling. The agent looked in the bag, closed it, and called Jose to come out to the gate. Another agent took the gate. Roberto walked up to the office with the agent and Jose.

Jose asked, "Where did you find so much money?"

Roberto closed the door then said, "I was approached by some drug-dealing boys over three years ago. Those boys wanted me to take some drugs across the border to a house in Douglas, Arizona. I told them, 'No, I don't like drugs.' Those boys almost beat me to death." He paused for some water. "A farmer and his wife picked me up out of a ditch and saved my life."

Jose said, "Did you repay them for their help?"

"Yes, I did. I gave them seven hundred dollars, then I walked toward town. It was two miles away. I saw two of the boys outside. The boys went inside, so I opened their door with my foot. The fight lasted for four minutes. As the boys were laying on the floor, I gagged them blindfolded and hog tied them." He drank some more water. "I found their drugs, took them out back, and burned them in the BBQ. The money I bagged and I am here." We counted eleven thousand one hundred dollars.

The CBP officer looked at the map of Mexico and pointed at the area just below Douglas.

Roberto said, "Yes, that is close."

Jose asked, "Did you kill them?"

"No sir. The boys were all tied up and alive when I left."

"Someone shot them and set the house on fire."

"That was not me, sir. Believe me. I don't have a gun. I didn't see any guns in their house."

"What are you going to do with the money?"

"I owe you for helping me get into the United States and giving me a place to stay. You also helped me find a job."

"We don't want your money, son. You hang onto it." Roberto put the money into a savings account and went back to work. The crew was happy to see him again.

The boss laughed and said, "We took bets after the first week of your vacation. "When will he return?" A pause. "I lost." Everyone laughed.

"I haven't seen the family in over three years. I want to go back again next year." Roberto chuckled. "I won't stay away that long again. Just a week."

"Back to work, guys. We have five cars to get out today if we can."

Roberto went to work with Doug and prepared a car for paint, then went to another car. "It needs rear end repair." The two removed the damaged bumper. It was holding the trunk closed. Doug opened the trunk and called the police. Jeff came over and pulled everyone away from the car. The police arrived with the medical examiner. The body was that of a man. The car was loaded up and taken by the police.

Jeff said, "We don't need any more bodies lying around." A little bit of chuckling. Everyone went back to work. Rob started working with Dave for the rest of the day. Roberto turned twenty-one. The body shop had a BBQ out back of the shop after working hours for him with some beer. The men's families were also invited. It was Friday. The birthday party was a great surprise for him. He didn't drink any beer.

The weekend was time for Roberto to relax. The shop was closed for this Saturday. Jose Rodriguez came over to talk to Roberto Garcia.

"Roberto, are you interested in becoming a CBP agent?"

"A cop?"

"No, a border patrol agent. There is a big difference."

"I don't know what to do to be an agent."

"We have a school for those wanting to work protecting our border from drugs and illegal immigrants."

"I can do that without becoming an agent."

"Yes, and get yourself killed? Become an agent or let us do our work, please, Roberto."

"I will do my best, Jose. I will love to be an agent. How long is the school?"

"Just six months. There are several classes of different types of training. The next classes start in a week."

"I need to talk to my boss."

"I already talked to Jeff. He said it is up to you. If you change your mind, you will always have a job with him."

Rob talked to Jeff and learned that Jose was right. He worked for three more days then went to the training in north El Paso. He checked in and started the training. Everyone went through situation problems and learned to recognize a drug dealer or someone carrying drugs north or money headed south.

The gun range was the next phase. Rob couldn't hit the target from twenty yards away. He needed a lot of help. No one laughed at him. The other prospective agents helped each other. He was able to hit the target when the training was finished. Six months went fast. The new CBP agents were sworn in to the border patrol agency. Roberto went to the foot traffic bridge with another agent. Rob looked close at all the working visa of everyone crossing.

The other agent said, "You don't have to look so hard."

"I have to get used to what I am looking for." He stopped the next person and held her there. "This is not you." He took the person to inspection and the visa check. She had been expelled a few months earlier. She was going to jail now for a while. Rob went back out to the gate and continued inspecting work permits.

Three weeks had passed, and he was out on the vehicle checking papers and asking many questions. His first week there, he brought three vehicles in for inspection. Mr. Rodriguez asked, "How did you know what vehicles to stop? Two of those vehicles come through almost every day."

"I can smell the drugs, or maybe it's the paper the drugs are wrapped in. I am not sure which one." Rob was serious.

"You have one hell of a nose." Then he laughed. "You saw what was found in those three vehicles. Over a million dollars street value in drugs."

Roberto went to the outbound traffic to see if his nose was still working. He was with another agent, James. The two were checking all outbound vehicles. Two weeks there, one driver was nervous. James pulled the car out and back for inspection. Another agent came over to help Roberto. Ten minutes had passed when Roberto pulled a car out for inspection. The couple could not answer his questions.

Another agent took his place. The car James pulled was carrying about two hundred thousand dollars in cash. James was now back on the line. Roberto was still helping the search of the pulled car. The back rests of all seats were filled with money. The seats were pulled open, and they found more money.

The car was sent to x-ray. The pictures showed more something in the vehicle. Mainly in the floor and ceiling. The car was taken back to inspection. When the ceiling material was removed, everyone started laughing. The top was stuffed with cocaine. The drug dealers forgot to pull all the drugs. The cash was one hundred fifty thousand dollars. The drugs were close to one and a half million dollars.

Another month on the outbound vehicle lanes, just minor problems. Roberto went back to the incoming pedestrian walkway.

The second week there, he stopped a young man. His papers were all good. He looked a little fat. His face matched.

He asked Roberto, "How do you like working here?"

"You are clear, sir, you can go." Rob thought that was strange to make a request like that. He turned toward the man and started running at him and tackled him. When the man hit the ground, he blew up. No parts of that man were recognizable. Roberto lay on the ground, unconscious. All gates were closed. The main office pushed the alarm. All border crossings were shut down from San Diego California to Brownsville, Texas, in less than five minutes.

The ambulance came and checked Roberto. He was alive but not moving. He was rushed to the hospital and rested in moderate but stable condition. His family was notified and brought to El Paso to see him. He was breathing on his own but in a coma. He remained that way for eleven days, then he opened his eyes. The border reopened, but everyone coming into the country would stop, be checked, and be searched by an agent with a dog there also.

There were two people working at the walkway. Every vehicle was searched with dogs. President Trump came to the hospital and visited Roberto Garcia. He was sitting up now with family around him. The president presented him with the medal of valor.

SAMMY BAKER

Sammy was born in Green River, Wyoming, on December 24, 1990.

She was the youngest of three female children. Her name was Samantha, but everyone called her Sammy. Their dad, John, was outnumbered. Everywhere he turned, one of the girls was there. He had a great job getting a good paycheck twice a month. Her mom was a stay-at-home mother. Sammy grew up learning from her older sisters. She was reading some books at four years old, way ahead of other children her age.

In 1997, at six, Sammy started the first grade. She was homeschooled by her mother and sisters. Sammy was in the first grade for about three months. She was sent up to the second grade just before Thanksgiving. Her sister Karen went to the fourth grade, and Bethel was in the fifth grade. Autumn was here, and the leaves were falling. The snow could not wait. Mid October, the first snow came, putting a blanket of three inches on the ground.

No more snow fell for a month, then the hard snow came on December first. Four days of snow laying down eleven inches. The snow was wet and heavy. The Baker's roof made some weird noises, and then part of it collapsed, dumping snow on the dining room. Mrs. Baker, Beverly, rushed the girls out of the house and over to the neighbor's house.

Beverly said, "Our roof collapsed. The dining room is full of snow."

The neighbor called the police and told them what happened. Thirty minutes later, the roof had a temporary cover on it. The snow was removed from the roof and inside the house. The next two days, neighbors came over and repaired the roof by replacing several rafters and repaired the dining room ceiling. To have such good neighbors is a must and a blessing. The cost of material was the Baker's only charge.

The father, John Baker, was thrilled for the help at no cost. Snow melt wires were put on the roof so most of the snow would melt and run off. The girls continued in school, and Mom went to work again at one of the restaurants in town. She was happy to get out of the house for a few hours each day. The school year came to an end. The girls all advanced to the next grade.

It was summertime, and the girls had plenty of time to relax and, in general, have fun. Young children spent a lot of time with their classmates and rode their bicycles a thousand miles and never left the city limits. Sammy got her first bicycle from the past Christmas. Her sisters, Karen, eleven, and Bethel, twelve, would ride with Samantha, Sammy, and have so much fun. The neighbor boys and girls, fourteen of them, protected each other everywhere they rode their bikes.

Dang it, summer was over, and there was another year of school to attend. Sammy was happy for another year of school. For some reason, she loved school more than most students. She was so much smarter than any of her classmates. The principal and teacher were thinking about sending her to the next grade. Karen was two years ahead of Sammy. The teacher, Marian, said, "She has proven that she needs to go up one more class." Sammy was moved to the fourth grade. Sammy's intelligence grew as she aged. Another year in the fifth grade—Sammy was doing great.

Another summer and a lot of fun. Beth and Karen were worried about Sammy passing both of them. No one knew where she was getting her intelligence, but it was there. She was now only ten years old but still one grade behind Karen, and Bethel would start high school next year.

Beth and Karen asked mom and dad, "Where did Sammy get her intelligence?"

Mom said, "We do not know. She didn't get it from me. Dad?"

"Look at my job, girls, I am just surviving."

Another summer came and went. School started, and Sammy was now in the seventh grade, staying one grade behind sister, Karen. Bethel went into high school. The school year went fast and then another summer. High school started for Karen. Two years later, Bethel graduated from high school. She wanted to be a teacher. Beth was ready for college. The year went fast. Her final GPA was the second highest with an average of 3.97. The SAT score was very good also.

Summer was great. Bethel received an academic scholarship at Weber State University, in Ogden, Utah. The scholarship was for full four years. Bethel was so happy she didn't know how to react.

Dad said, "Honey, take it. We can help you during the summer, but you will have to work also. We do not have much money to help." Sammy and Karen worked during the summer also and mailed their earnings to Bethel.

"Thank you, sis, Mom, and Dad." Beth moved to Ogden, Utah, and found an apartment with two other girls. Their rent was much more manageable with three girls working. Karen started her senior year of high school. She and Sammy found part-time jobs to help Bethel. Karen's year went good for her. She graduated as valedictorian. She outdid Beth with a GPA of 3.985. Her SAT was almost perfect.

She got a letter from Idaho Falls. The return address was University of Idaho. "We would appreciate your visit to our university. Please give us a call. Thank you very much, university vice president." The phone number was on the letter

"Mom, Dad, what do I do? I haven't saved any money. I don't want to tell them no."

Karen was excited to receive their letter. Karen called the number the next day. The secretary answered the phone and transferred the line to the recruiter. "Is this Miss Karen Baker?"

"Yes, sir." She was nervous. He noticed it in her voice.

"Be calm, Miss Baker. Would you be interested on attending our university? We are not a large school, but we have a good variety of academic classes."

Karen said, "I am wanting to become a teacher somewhere. Elementary or high school."

"We will be able to accommodate your request. Would you be interested in a full four scholarship?"

Through her tears, she managed to say yes.

"Thank you, Miss Baker. I will be sending you a bus ticket. Pack the clothes you will need, and we will see you soon."

Bethel finished her first year and found a full-time summer job. She called home and talked for twenty-five minutes. "I have a full-time job for the summer. I have to go to work now. Call you again this weekend."

Mom told her, "Karen is going to University of Idaho."

"Good for her. Give my love to Dad and sisters."

Karen packed her clothes and waited for the bus ticket. Dad gave her one hundred dollars, and Sammy added thirty-three more dollars. Mom's money was used for food. Karen gave everyone a hug and said, "Thank you very much. I will find a job when I get to the school."

Sammy started her summer job. At fourteen, she could only work five hours a day, so she was working two jobs. She had to sneak in the second job. Karen found a place to stay before school started, then she could get a dorm room. Her job was working with a day care, preschool class. Low wages, but that was the only job available. Mid July, she found another job. She was working both jobs until school started.

Samantha started her last year of high school, and Karen started her first year of college in Idaho Falls. Dad and Mom sent what they could. It was split between Beth and Karen. Sammy was working through the school year. With her summer jobs and after-school job, she managed to send three hundred dollars to her sisters. One hundred fifty dollars each. Samantha's last high school year came to an end.

Sammy was valedictorian with a GPA of 3.99. Her SAT was two points short of perfect. After graduation, Sammy received a four-year academic scholarship to become a teacher at the University of Wyoming in Cheyenne.

Sammy talked to her sisters and mom. "I am not interested in being a teacher, Mom. I am only fifteen."

Mom asked, "Well, what is on your mind?"

"I don't know. I am too young to be teaching. Give me a few years."

Dad said, "You will be nineteen after graduation. Mom and I started teaching at eighteen. Our first student was your sister, Beth." Everyone laughed. "Changing diapers choked me up." More laughter.

The next year, Sammy went to college at the University of Wyoming. She told the school her age.

The president said, "That is fine with us." Samantha started her first year of college. She still studied hard to get good grades. She found a part-time job to help pay for her needs. She worked hard and studied harder. Beth and Karen sent Samantha some money each month because they knew she was not old enough to get a better after-school job.

Her class grades were 3.99 to 4.00. She amazed all the staff and instructors. Her first semester ended. Samantha wanted to go home and start over in two years.

Some of her classmates said, "Please don't quit, Sam. You are very young, but you are smarter than anyone else. We are building ourselves off your enthusiasm for getting such high grades. We need you." Sam went to her job during the winter holidays. She needed the money.

The second semester started, and she was ready. Sam also worked when she could. She was working at a restaurant on weekends. The air national guard was not far away. An airman ordered supper, and Sam served their food. He said thank you, then he grabbed her arm. "Will you go out with me?" Another waitress rushed over there. He would not let go of her arm. Sam said, "Let me go."

"Answer me."

The other waitress said, "Let her go. If you don't, she will kick your ass all the way back to your base. She is a fourth-degree black belt."

He let go and finished his dinner. He didn't leave a tip. The other waitresses gave her what he should have tipped her. He came back a few weeks later. Sammy would not serve him even though that was her table. She went to the table. "If you are not going to leave me a tip, then get out and eat somewhere else. I am trying to work my way through college. Every little bit helps me."

He got up and moved to another table.

The manager went over to him and said, "Don't ever grab one of my waitresses again, okay?"

He didn't say anything, just got up and left the restaurant. We never saw him again that semester. Summertime came, and she started working full time at the restaurant during the day shift. Samantha was a very good waitress. A lot of the military and spouse came in there for a break from home cooking.

Sam was happy to serve them. She always got a decent tip. The little children would get an ice cream cone after eating. A few days passed, and the same airman came in with some friends. The group sat down in one of Samantha's tables. She walked over there and brought menus. "Would you like something to drink?"

Three boys said, "Beer, please."

The jerk said, "I would like your breast milk." She didn't hesitate. She hit his nose and broke it. Then she said, "Get out. You are banned from this restaurant."

His sergeant heard his words and walked over there. "Corporal, you are way out of line. Get out. The rest of you are all too young to be drinking beer. If you want soda and some food, fine." The other boys ordered a burger and fries with coke. A few minutes later, she brought their food. One of them asked, "Do you date men?"

"Not yet, I am only sixteen."

"Oh my gosh. I thought you were in college."

"I am, I finished high school at fifteen." Their jaws dropped. The boys left her twenty dollars tip.

She smiled and said, "Thank you, gentlemen." The rest of the summer went to fast, but she did make two thousand dollars in wages. The tips were close to five hundred dollars. For a sixteen-year-old girl, she felt good.

She asked the head waitress, "Do I have to pay taxes on this money?"

"Unfortunately, yes, honey. Just keep your record of pay through December. We can help you come tax time." She started her second year. Bethel started her senior year. She was really excited. Her GPA to this point was 3.88. Karen was receiving good grades also. She had a GPA of 3.85. Samantha had called home several times during the summer. She also called her sisters. She told them that she has plenty of cash to get her through this year. "I will try to be at your graduation, Beth."

She said, "Don't lose any work time, sis. Mom and Dad will send you some pictures." A pause. "Oh gosh, Sammy, I am so excited."

"I am excited for you too, sis." Samantha started her second year; Karen started her third year. Sammy worked part time and weekends. Mid November, she saw that boy standing close to the restaurant. She went back in the restaurant and waited for one of the other girls to get off.

Janet asked, "I thought you were going back to school?"

"That boy is out there. I do not trust him." Janet called the owner, Fred. He went outside and looked at him. Sammy came out, and Fred drove her to the campus. "Thank you, Fred."

He said, "I will take you home every day you work."

Sammy said, "I am going to stay on campus until summer. I have some money in reserve."

Fred laughed, "But we need you." Fred talked to the commander about "one of your men stalking one of my waitresses." A week later, that boy was transferred to the east coast. Fred went to the campus and talked to Sammy.

She said, "I will work on the weekends until summer." Fred agreed. Christmas vacation time. Sammy went home for this time off. She was already registered for the next semester. Her sisters were also home for this Christmas. Samantha would be seventeen.

Beth asked Sammy, "How many 4.0 grades do you have?"

"I have one 3.98. That's my lowest grade. I am not bragging, sis. You are doing great also. Keep up your high grades. I am proud of both of you."

Mom said, "Quit talking school. Is anyone hungry?" They sat down and had a great Christmas dinner and relaxed for a couple days. Samantha talked about her job and the boy that was stalking her.

"He was transferred to the east coast. I hope he stays there." The girls stayed through New Year's Day then headed to their college.

Samantha rode the bus to university of Wyoming on snow-covered roads. She got back to her dorm room. Everyone was talking about a shooting. She didn't pay any attention until her roommate said, "That soldier boy came back looking for you. The campus security confronted him. He pulled a gun and security shot and killed him. One security man was wounded."

Sammy cried. "I am sorry for the security man. How is he doing?"

Donna said, "He is fine. Just a minor wound."

"Any wound is not minor." The next day, she went to security office.

She talked to them and the man who was wounded.

The captain said, "Not to worry. We are all fine. We were just doing our job." Sammy went back to her room and sat for a while, then went to talk to the dean.

After a long talk, she said, "I will stay and finish my college here."

Samantha took her income papers to the restaurant and got help filing her taxes. She only paid forty-eight dollars. Her second year was coming to an end. She was enjoying school more. Now she was thinking about her major. *I guess I will be a teacher*, she was thinking. Sammy wanted to go to Bethel's graduation. She called her.

Beth said, "Don't worry, sis. I understand. I will send you some pictures."

Sammy went to work at the restaurant and started working full time. The National Guard families knew what happened. That incident didn't keep them from coming to the restaurant a couple of times a month.

Bethel graduated with high grades. She was offered a teaching position in New Mexico. Bethel took the job. She was happy to get out of Utah and Wyoming. Beth went to the elementary school. She would be teaching the fifth grade for her internship year. Her pay wouldn't start until September, so she went looking for a job close to the school in Santa Fe.

There were plenty of jobs available but decided to go home first and spend time with family for most of the summer.

Karen and Samantha took two weeks off and went home. The three, now young ladies, had a lot of fun. They visited all their regular stops and their classmates. Some moved away, and some married after school. A short marriage, then divorce for one couple. Samantha's best friend went to a junior college for two years and became a nurse. Sammy found that she was in Las Vegas Hospital in pediatric care.

Samantha went back to college and back to work. Karen went back to school also. She had one more year then start looking for a teaching position. She called Samantha. The two talked for an hour.

Karen said, "I have to go to work. Talk again later. Love you, sis."

Samantha said, "I love you too." Sammy had to go to work also. She got in ten weeks of work. She met those three good men several times during the summer. Not one of them mentioned the lost soul. He had a bad attitude on life. Samantha had a break and sat down with the men.

They knew how old she was, so they just enjoyed talking with her. Her intelligence intrigued them.

Back to school. The third year started, and Samantha was getting excited, knowing she had this year and then one more. She kept a better record of her pay this year. The holidays were here. Another break from classes. One more semester for this school year. Karen called home and talked for over an hour. Samantha couldn't get through to Mom and Dad, so she called Karen. Her line was busy also.

Sammy called Bethel. The two talked for a while, then she called home again. She talked to Mom and Dad for a short while.

"I will be home this coming summer. I want to see pictures of Karen. I just might be able to go to Idaho this year for her graduation. I am disappointed I couldn't watch Bethel graduate."

"Call later, honey. We love you and Karen."

June 2009 came up fast, and Karen's graduation was real close.

Samantha finished her classes, had a flight to Idaho Falls, and arrived two days before graduation. Karen and Samantha could pass for twins. Bethal was three inches taller than her sisters. Samantha walked on the campus. She started to asked where Karen was. One of her classmates said, "Hey, Karen, are you as excited as I am?"

Karen walked out and said, "Yes, I am." Her friend, Sally, looked in the direction of Karen's voice then looked back at Samantha, pointing at both of them. The two laughed.

Sally asked, "Are you twins?"

Karen said, "No this is my younger sister. She will graduate next year."

Mom and Dad showed up with Bethel. Her internship went great. She liked New Mexico. She asked Mom and Dad to move there. She would find them a house. Dad said, "No, honey. We grew up here from babies. I don't think we could live anywhere else. Beth rented two rooms close to the graduation ceremony."

Two days later, Karen walked up and received her bachelor's degree. Another teacher of the future. Dad said, "Well, Sam, are you ready to become number three?"

"No, Dad. I am not going to finish school. I found an army man at the national guard unit." She paused about thirty seconds, then she started laughing. Dad was ready to strangle her.

"Don't you ever do that to me. I have a weak heart." Then he laughed. Sam took two weeks off to spend time with the family and friends. Samantha went back to Cheyenne and back to work. Karen put her resume out for higher. She got a request to come back to Idaho Falls and teach English in their high school.

She said, "I will see you in a few days." Beth went looking in Nevada. She got a request at the school in Hawthorne, Nevada. She looked for it. She found the town in the middle of nowhere.

She said, "Yes, I will be there in a week, I hope." She had a car, so she drove there. The trip took her four days. When she got there, she was told that she will be teaching a lot of military students mixed with civilian kids.

"That is okay with me. They are all humans, aren't they?" The teachers all laughed along with the principal.

He said, "You will do good here. Do you gamble?"

"For money? I haven't yet."

Samantha started her last year at University of Wyoming. She didn't slow down. Her grades were the top of the class. 3.99/4.0. Karen was halfway through her internship. She was doing great and really getting used to teaching. That first year is the hardest for a new teacher. Samantha finished her first half of her last year of college. She called home and talked for about a half hour to Mom and Dad.

"Now I know how Beth and Karen felt when their last half year comes up. The excitement runs through my body."

Dad said, "We never made it as far as you and your sisters have."

Mom said, "We are so proud of all three of you girls. Our hearts are filled with pride, Sammy." She started crying. "We love you, honey. Finish your last semester, baby."

"I will, Mom, Dad. I love you both. I am starting to cry. Bye for now. I will call later." Sam went to her room and did some more studying. She was nineteen now and ready to finish her last semester. The last few months went slow but finally came to an end. The last week was time to relax and finish the final tests. Samantha was not worried. Her grades were the top of the class. No other student could catch up to her.

The final tests were given and now they were waiting to find out what their grades are. Samantha Baker finished as the valedictorian. Her GPA was 3.999.

Samantha's family showed up for her graduation. She was thrilled. Beth and Karen split the cost of three rooms. Bethel brought her boyfriend, Allen. The day came and a lot of talk, then the students received their bachelor's degree. Samantha took two weeks off then put out her resume. Weber State called her. The president didn't want to wait for the mail to go through. She might get another offer. Her grades impressed them.

Samantha said, "I will be there tomorrow." She rode the bus. She didn't have a car yet. She needed a driver's license first. She arrived at Weber State and talked to some of the teachers and the upper staff. She was asked to teach English.

"Yes, I will. Thank you for the offer. This is still my first year. I am only nineteen." Some weird looks on their faces.

She said, "You don't want a child teaching your students. If so, I will go elsewhere." She stood up and started to walk out.

The dean said, "We didn't realize you were so young. Wait a few minutes, okay?"

He made three calls. The last one was a jackpot for Samantha.

The dean said, "There is an opening at the high school on Hill Air Force Base. Are you interested?"

Samantha laughed. "That is good. I went through college in Cayenne, around three hundred army national guard. I think I can handle some high school military brats."

She got registered on the base and would have a house on base. She would be teaching English. Samantha called home and told them what happened. "I will be teaching English on an Air Force base. Now I need a car. I will be able to get one after school starts. I will be home for a while in a couple days, Mom."

"We will be waiting." Two days later, Sammy showed up on their front steps. The whole family was there.

Bethel had a husband and two sons. Karen had a daughter. She was not married. Her daughters' father left the area. Just a playboy on the run. Sammy didn't have anyone. She didn't want a man yet. She was only nineteen.

"I am here, Mom. How is everyone doing?"

"We are fine. I am happy you made the trip here."

"Where is my dad?"

"Working. He will be home in an hour."

"I guess I will wait for him." Then she laughed.

Dad finally got home. He was surprised and happy to see his children. All three daughters were there. Two daughters had children. Jim was so happy he started crying. He was in his fifties. Everyone went into the kitchen, and Mom fixed some drinks for the adults. The children had sodas. Dad was so happy to see his children. All three were schoolteachers. The three girls sent a monthly allotment to their Mom and Dad. One thousand dollars a month each.

Their mom and dad were getting thirty-six thousand dollars a year, plus their working pay put them over fifty thousand dollars each year. Their parents were so happy they didn't know what to say.

Beth said, "You scrimped and scratched to put us through school. We knew it was time to pay you back. This money is on us, Mom and Dad." For the next ten years, their parents received three thousand dollars each month without fail.

Their dad was injured at work. He went on disability. The company paid him twenty thousand dollars. The girls did not slow down on their monthly allotments. The three girls' pay combined was making over one hundred fifty thousand dollars each year. Their parents were getting thirty-six thousand dollars each year. Mom quit working, unless she got bored sitting at home, which was all the time.

Samantha finally found a man that had a stable job. He was a history teacher at Hill Air Force Base. The two liked each other very much. The two dated for several months. Sammy was hoping for a proposal. Five months later, he proposed to Samantha. She didn't wait. "Yes, honey." I wanted to be sure in my mind that this is what I really wanted to do. I told myself, yes. I love you, honey, and I always will," Samantha cried.

Terry and Sammy set a date. July 1. The family had part of the summer off. Everyone prepared for the wedding. Six days later, the wedding was completed and everyone was happy. Terry and Samantha were married.

After a few days, the two were at their new home. Samantha was happy, and her husband was a very intelligent man. Almost as smart as her. Their house was off base in Clearfield, Utah.

SHEILA

Robby Dees Joined the Navy in 1953. He went through boot camp in San Diego. He was the youngest of seven children. His older brothers and sisters finished college before he was born. He came out of boot camp as an EN (E-3). He was stationed right in the naval station in the engine overhaul department. He had the weekend off, so he rode the bus to downtown San Diego. He saw lots of sex clubs, but he wasn't interested. Rob was on his way back to the base when he saw this young girl sitting on a bus stop bench, crying.

"What is wrong, miss? Is there any way I can help you?"

With tears in her eyes, she said, "I am hungry and I don't have any money."

"What would you like to eat? I will buy it for you. There is a restaurant just down the street." She got up and followed him to the restaurant. The two walked in and set down.

The manager said, "Get her out of my business."

"We just want something to eat. Look at her. She is starving." He grabbed Rob's arm. Rob hit him twice, putting him on his butt.

"Come on, Sheila. We will find another place to eat."

"Wait. What do you want to eat?"

"Two burgers with fries and two Cokes please." The cook started cooking the food. The manager brought out the Cokes. "I am six feet, four inches tall. I have never been dropped before with just two hits. I was a heavyweight boxer in the Marines for eight years."

"Sorry, sir. You toughed my wrong side. I am a second-degree black belt in karate." He brought the burgers and fries.

"Miss, slow down on your eating. You will make yourself sick." Rob slid his soda over to her. She emptied her glass. She washed down the food and then took another bite of the burger. Rob cut his in half and ate it slowly. She finished her burger and fries. She looked at Rob's burger half. He slid it over to her.

Rob said, "Slow down. No one will take it from you. She ate all but one bite. Rob ate the last bite.

"Thank you, sir. I was hungry."

"Yes, we saw that. Now what do you want to do?"

"I need to go to my room. Just down the street." Rob walked with her to an alley.

She said, "Thank you, sir. I will be fine now."

"That is not a safe place to stay. Come with me. I have some friends that might help you get off the street into a warm house and your own room. Are you interested?"

She held Rob and asked, "Will those people do that for me?"

"I think so. Taxi." They rode to Don's parents' house. Don was there also. Rob knocked on the door. Don opened it. "Come in, Rob. Who is your friend?"

"Her name is Sheila. I don't normally pick up strangers, but I saw her crying. I took her to eat. She was hungry. If I am off base, just let me know. She was sleeping in an alley. Is there any chance she can stay here for a while until I can find her another place to stay?"

"Where are your parents, Sheila?"

She said, "My parents kicked me out two weeks ago. I reached fourteen, and they said, 'Get out. You are on your own.'"

June asked, "Kicked out or run away?"

She started crying. "Come on, Sheila. I will find a place for you to stay. There is a motel close by. I can put you up there for a week."

"Robby, I didn't say no. I am just...where are your parents?"

"My ex-parents live in Los Vegas. I bummed a ride to San Diego, but I ran out of money."

June said, "Come with me. Get out of those dirty clothes and put these on. I will wash them for you. The shower is next door. Clean your body and hair." June came into the living room. "What is her last name?"

"She said it is, Bailey. Look in her clothes." Sheila came out for a minute. "Here is my school ID card. That is all I have. Thank you all for letting me stay here a while." She went into the shower and washed her hair and body real good. After getting dried off and dressed, she came out and said, "Thank you very much. I will work for you while I am here." She went to her room and went to bed. She was asleep in a minute.

Tom said, "I know you are wary about a total stranger honey, but be patient. I will see if I can locate her parents. It is illegal to kick a child out of the house, but I know it happens." Tom was retired Navy, so he drove up to Las Vegas. He asked around, but no one knew the Baileys. Two days there and tired of looking, he decided to do some gambling. He lost sixty dollars.

A young man came to Tom. "You are looking for Mike and Sherl Bailey. They are standing over there. He owns this casino."

Tom walked to Mike and asked, "Why did you kick your daughter out of your house?"

"She became a pain in the rear. Never doing her chores. Where is she?"

"Do you really care? She almost starved to death. Sheila is doing better, but she needs some support from you two. She wants twenty thousand dollars."

"Get out of here!"

"Do you want to go to jail?"

Mike went into the office and came back with five thousand dollars. "This is all I can afford. We are almost broke. Please don't come back."

Tom drove back to San Diego and talked to Sheila. "I found your parents. Apparently you didn't like doing your chores—is that right?"

She started crying and walked out of the house. Tom grabbed her and brought her back into his house.

"I didn't say you could go. Your dad gave me five thousand dollars to give to you, but you have to do your chores here." He smiled and handed her a package. Sheila looked in and saw a lot of money. "Thank you, sir." Don and Rob went to Don's house after the work was done for the day. The third class test would be in a week. Rob wanted to be an electrician's mate. He was working as an engineman at the present. Time for the test. Don and Rob were handed their test.

Rob said, "I asked for an electrician's test."

The proctor said, "This is what I was sent. It's not up to me." Robby took the test. He was done in forty-five minutes. He dropped the test on the proctor's desk and walked out.

Rob talked to the division officer. "I want to be an electrician. Why did you give me an engineman test?"

"I need enginemen, not electricians."

"It is not up to you to decide what a person wants."

"I am your division officer. Don't argue with me." Rob left and talked to the master chief. He took Rob to the executive officer.

Rob said, "Sir, I want to be an electrician, not an engineman. I requested a test for electrician's mate. My DO said he doesn't want electricians."

The XO went to the engine shop. He spent thirty minutes yelling at the division officer. "Order an electrician's mate third class test for Mr. Dees now." The test came in two days later. Robby took the test. He was done in thirty-eight minutes.

The proctor asked, "You still have over an hour to check your answers."

"I did check my answers. I am done, sir." The test was sent in. A week had passed when an officer came to the base and talked to the commander asking about E-3 Robby Dees. "What does he want to be?"

"That's been taken care of, Lieutenant."

"That is why I am here, Captain. He passed both tests. He only missed two questions on the engineman test. None on the electrician's mate test. Two times one hundred fifty, what is his IQ level?"

"We don't check IQ on anyone." The captain laughed. "Probably higher than ours."

Rob bought a house in the same housing area as the Franks. Just a block away. Rob went up to the Franks' house and talked to Sheila. She was still fourteen for another month. She was ready to move. Sheila thanked Tom and June for their help. She gave them one thousand dollars. Sheila spent some money on new clothes. Rob bought her some cookbooks. Sheila was happy to be living with the person who saved her from starving.

She asked Rob, "Honey, I want to know what lovemaking feels like. I have never had any sex." Everything needed was moved into their house. Rob had to help her learn how to cook. She was learning fast. Rob called his mom. His father is twenty-five years older than his mom. "Come down here mom. I bought a house close to the base. I miss your company. I have a friend living with me. She is not a good cook. Would you help me teach her how to cook?"

"I will fly down. I will let you know my flight and time I will be there, okay, honey? I am tired of this ice box temperature."

"Thank you, Mom. I love you." The next day, Petty Officer third class Robby Dees went to the airport and picked up his mom. Sheila went with him. Rob's transportation was a '54 Dodge pickup.

"Thank you, Mom, for coming down here. This is Sheila. Sheila, my mom, Dorothy." Rob drove back to his house. "I am off for the day. Pick your room, Mom. You have two to choose from."

"These are new beds. Did you get any bedding for them?"

"Oh yes, Mom. The sheets and blankets are in the closet with pillows."

Sheila said, "I will help you make up your bed. We can talk?" An hour of talking and Dorothy accepted her as a daughter. Even though Sheila was so young, Dorothy didn't say anything to cause the separation of Sheila and her son. The two were very much in love. She thought about her late husband and the age difference between them.

The next advancement tests were just a day away. Rob had been working for the base electrical department since he made third class. The second class test didn't slow him down much. This test took Rob forty-eight minutes to complete the test. In 1954, Sheila turned fifteen and wanted a baby.

Dorothy said, "Please wait another year, honey. You have plenty of life to live and have children." Sheila looked disappointed but accepted her words. She didn't want to make her angry. Rob was advanced to second-class petty officer. Six more months passed, and it was time for the first-class test.

His friend, Don, also took the first-class engineman test but didn't advance. Rob was now a first-class electrician's mate. Only two and a half years in the Navy and moving up the chain. He was now supervisor for his shop. Sheila was now pregnant. She waited eight months before getting pregnant. Rob got transferred to a carrier. The ship would be in port for another four months.

In 1955, Rob took one week leave and saw the delivery of their son. His mom taught the new parents how to take care of their son, David John. Sheila turned sixteen two months before her baby was born.

Rob went to sea finally and headed for the Philippines to relieve the other ships. The transfer was fast, and the other ships were on their way home.

The ship visited several ports. He did plenty of shopping. Nine months out and now it was time to head home. Back at home, he brought all the things he purchased off the ship and took them home. Their son was now one year old. He had to get his son's love. "I didn't take the chiefs test. I am going to get out. I have five months left, then I will be home every night."

August 1956, Rob walked off the ship and never looked back. Robby and family went north, and he talked to General Electric for a job.

TERRI AND JERRI

Twin girls born mid May 1999 in Normal, Illinois, to a mid-income family. Terri and Jerri grew up a couple of happy girls. The Mangrum family were having fun during the summers. Mom, Karen, and dad, Gary, planed trips south to go fishing or just go camping somewhere. With three older children, the twins had someone to look up to.

In 2005, Jerri and Terri started the first grade. The two girls competed against each other to be the best all the way through elementary school.

Being the youngest of the family, their two older brothers and sister were out of school now. Connie found a job, and the boys left the state looking for work elsewhere.

Karen took the twins to a karate class every Saturday. Their karate training started when the girls went into the fourth grade. Their instructor said, "This is for self-defense only. If you get caught beating anyone up for no reason, I will cancel your training." The girls agreed and kept practicing all the way through high school. Both girls left high school with a black belt in karate.

Terri and Jerri worked hard on learning everything they could in school. Competing against each other through high school, it put them at the top of their class all four years. Terri graduated with a GPA of 3.994, and Jerry finished with a 3.9939. Both girls took the SAT and was accepted to the university of Illinois. Terri and Jerri had all four years of college paid for by the state.

Both girls studied hard and at the end of the first year, their grades were top of their classes. The girls found a karate class close to the college and signed up for it. The girls went home for part of the summer and spent time with the family. Back at the college, their jobs were still there. The money bought them the required feminine things and food during the summer. Their second year started, and both girls worked part time during the school year.

The girls went home this year for Christmas. Their parents were so happy to see the twins. Dad asked, "What is your major? What do you want to be after graduating?"

Both girls said, "They were not sure."

Mom said, "It is time to start thinking about it, honey."

Jerri said, "I know, Mama, but what makes good money with the most time off?" Then she laughed.

Terri said, "A teacher gets a good paycheck with summers off. I think that is my choice."

Jerri said, "I agree with you, sis. I guess I will be a teacher also." The second year came to an end; the twins went home for a month of the summer. Still taking karate classes during the summer, both girls advanced to a second-degree black belt.

They went back to work and prepared for their third year. With books purchased, studying was the main thing on their minds. Neither one was trying to outdo the other, just get good grades. So far, both girls were the top of their class. The first semester ended, and there was some winter rest for both of them, but each of them worked part time during the holidays.

The third year came to an end, and they were home again for the summer. Both girls were home for most of the summer.

Dad said, "It is about time you two spent more time home this year. We miss you girls so much. We are not young anymore." He had tears in his eyes.

Mom said, "Thank you for coming home. Just relax for a while and enjoy the summer. We are so proud of both of you. Don't give up your dream, honey. We will be at your graduation. We love you girls."

Back to school in August, the twins went back to work before school started and back to karate training. Their father gave them two thousand dollars so they would not have to work so hard.

With their last year in session, they were back to the grindstone and keeping their grades up. The year went fast, and now it was time for their graduation from college. Their parents, both brothers and sister, were all there for their graduation from college. Two very happy girls. Graduation ceremonies went great. The two girls were valedictorians. Terri talked first, and Jerri finished their talk. Their talk lasted thirty-two minutes.

After receiving their degrees, the family went home and celebrated with a couple of drinks. A few days both girls sent their resume out to all the local schools. Every school wanted them. Terri went to the local high school to teach math.

Jerri went to teach the fifth grade at the closest school to her parents' home. She wanted to help her parents live with funds to enjoy their last few years. Terri said she would help them also. She would match Jerri's funds. The girls decided on one thousand five hundred dollars each every month. Three thousand dollars for their parents would help them enjoy their retirement. The first check from their daughters brought tears to their parents' eyes.

The first year, their parents put almost half of the money into a fidelity account. The money continued for the next three years. The girls' parents said to stop the money. "We are doing fine without your money. We have put some of the money into a bank account. You need to do the same. We love you both, but think about yourself first."

Jerri said, "We are doing that. Our fidelity account is getting larger."

Mom said, "Well, add more to your account. We are fine without your extra help. We appreciate your help, honey, but please think about yourself first." The oldest boy, Jake, landed a better job with the CIA. He was very smart and put his brain to work. He was working as a city police officer but said yes to the new job.

Jake disappeared for several months. When he got home, he told his parents, "My job is secret. Please don't ask me about what I do, Dad."

Fred was now trying to get back to college. He finished one year but couldn't save enough money to continue in school. Jerri said she would help him finish his college. Terri also donated some money. He wanted to be a finance officer.

The twins started their third year teaching. Some of their monthly excess money paid for Fred's school, and the rest went into their fidelity account. Big brother was so happy that his little sisters were helping him finish college. He promised them he would finish and pay them back somehow. Terri said, "Don't rob a bank," then laughed.

"The thought never entered my mind, sis." He laughed. "After I graduate, if I can get a job with the mafia." Everyone laughed.

Jake said, "Don't cause me to come hunting you, brother. I do not know what I would do." Then he started laughing. "Once you graduate, be careful on the job you take, Fred. I would hate to have the government looking for you."

Jake was gone again. This time, nobody saw him for over a year. The worst thoughts ran through the families' minds. Dad said to Fred, "Do not let Jake's disappearance keep you from your schooling. Keep your grades up, son. Let me do the worrying." Gary had tears in his eyes. Karen held him, and her eyes filled up with tears also.

A few days later, Jake showed up. "Mom, Dad, please don't worry. I resigned from the CIA. I am going to find a different type of a job. I can't tell you where I have been, but I will not be going anywhere anymore except to local job hunting. The relief of Jake being home brought tears of joy to everyone's eyes. Jake found a job with the city police department again.

Fred finished his third year with high grades. The twins were ready to start their fourth year teaching at local schools. Jake was happy to be home every night. His parents were happy too. Jake was courting a woman that he went through school with. He proposed to Tammy. She said yes. He had a ring and put it on her finger. Their wedding was set for three weeks away.

Everyone was resting during summer and waiting for Jake and Tammy's wedding. July 8, 2025, was just one week away. The excitement was running high in everyone, especially Jake. He was thirty-six years old. The invitations went out earlier. No one turned them down. Tammy's parents and her local relatives said they would be there. Jake, Jacob, was pulled away four days before the wedding.

Tammy and Jake's parents met a week earlier. All the women in both families took Tammy to find a wedding dress. Terri and Jerri brought some extra money but didn't let anyone know. There were so many choices but very little money from Tammy's family. Tammy tried on a beautiful dress. The price was one thousand, three hundred dollars.

Her mom looked at her sister and aunt. Jerri brought eight hundred dollars out of her purse, and Terri matched that amount. Terri took the sixteen hundred dollars and gave it to Tammy's mom, Joan.

She looked at the girls and gave them a hug with tears in her eyes. "Thank you so very much, but this is too much."

Karen said, "Use that money for the reception cost after the wedding. Here is another five hundred dollars."

The wedding cake was already ordered, and the food will be there also. The reception was set next to the church. Everyone started arriving for the wedding. Jake was up front by the priest waiting for Tammy. Her dad was waiting outside the room where she was getting dressed and had a drink while in the room. Both moms were in the room with her.

The mothers came out and went up front and sat down. Tammy came out and walked up front with her dad. The flower girl was in front, and the ringbearer followed the bridesmaid. Tammy arrived next to the priest, and Dad sat down. He said yes to the question from the priest. A few minutes passed, and both placed the rings on each other's ring finger.

The priest said, "I would like to introduce everyone to Mr. and Mrs. Jacob Mangrum." Everyone moved to the reception room. The cake was three layers. The newlyweds cut the cake and fed each other, then everyone got a piece of cake with ice cream for the children. A lot of pictures were taken by both families. There were lots of drinks for adults.

The reception came to an end, and everyone headed home. We didn't see Jake or Tammy for several days. Now both of them had to go back to work. With more on his mind, safety was more important now that he has a wife and a baby on the way. On his days off,

Jake started looking for a safer job. Nothing was available yet, but he would keep looking. Back to his police officer position and street job.

Summer was still here. Jerri went shopping for a three-wheel motorcycle. The Can Am interested her. She bought a light-blue motorcycle. Terri was with her. She drove her car home, while Jerri rode her Can Am home. Her dad said, "Are you crazy, honey? Those bikes are dangerous."

"Dad, this has three wheels on the ground. It is much safer than a regular two-wheel motorcycle."

He said, "Take me for a ride." He then laughed. Jerri went for a few miles then back home. "That is the smoothest bike ride I have ever been on. I will let you keep it, honey."

"Well, thank you, Dad. I had no plans of getting rid of it." Both girls had boyfriends, but neither man seemed to be really serious. Terri went for a ride with Jerri and decided to buy one also. Terri rode with Jerri to the dealer ship of Can Am motor cycles. The salesman looked and said, "Which one are you?"

"I am Terri. I want that gray one." No hesitation.

The salesman just stood there, kinda shocked. "Are you going to sell me that bike, or shall I get another salesman?"

"Yes, ma'am, follow me and we can do the paperwork." Thirty-five minutes had passed, and the papers were all done. Terri paid cash for the Can Am three-wheel bike. Twenty-two thousand dollars. Their regular driver's license was all that is required for these vehicles. No seatbelts. Just a helmet and warm clothing.

When the girls got home, their parents just shook their heads.

"Be very safe, girls," Mom said. "My turn for a ride. Whom do I ride with?" Mom rode with Jerri, and Dad rode with Terri. The riders went forty miles to a restaurant that was a motorcycle gang hangout. Dad was nervous. There was close to thirty Harleys parked out front. "Don't worry, Mom, Dad, we have been here before. These guys are all nice people."

Inside, a man said, "Here are those beautiful women. Are those your parents? Welcome, sir, ma'am." They ordered some lunch, ate, then headed home. Gary and Karen felt better once they were on their way out of the area.

Back home, Terri said, "Dad, those people are not the Hell's Angels. Relax, Mom. Jerri and I have been there several times. That group of riders have been in the area many years. They are all nice men and women."

Jerri and Terri packed up some clothes. Their trip would take them several hundred miles round trip. Traveling from Normal, Illinois, to the Atlantic Coast, their trip would be long. They wanted to go to Erie, Pennsylvania, and do some fishing plus camping. Not wanting to go alone, the girls went to the motorcycle gang and talked to some of the men with wives. Most of them had good jobs.

Only two men were willing to go with them. Both of them were single. Stan and Allen said, "We will go," but they didn't have much money. The girls canceled their trip for this year. School was about to start now, so both girls got ready for another year teaching.

Fred started his last year of college with good grades to this point. Fred had married after high school, but it only lasted five months. She wanted out, so Fred gave in, and the two filed for an annulment. Now finishing his last year of college, he was really happy. His last year came to an end, and the whole family went to his graduation.

When he received his bachelor's degree, he cried. A long time coming. His ex-wife was there. She said, "I am happy for you, honey. Will you give me another chance?"

Fred said, "Get the hell away from me. No!" Fred was dating one of the students seeking the same profession. Fred and Mary talked about their future. Fred said, "Maybe two years with a company, then we can have the training to start our own business." Mary agreed.

After a few months working, Fred invited Mary out for dinner. The two were sharing an apartment together. They were working for different companies; their meeting was after work. He had already purchased a ring for engagement and wedding band. At the restaurant, their food was ordered, and Fred went to the bathroom.

When he got back, Mary was gone. He almost started crying. The waitress said, "She went to the bathroom." Fred took a deep breath and wiped his eyes and tried to look confident. Mary came out; Fred got up and helped her seat herself. He then reached into his pocket and went onto one knee.

Mary smiled and stood up. Fred proposed to her. She said, "Yes, sweetie, yes yes!" Fred stood up and put the ring on her finger. The two kissed and held each other. A few people applauded them. Their supper arrived, and the two ate sitting very close to each other. The next morning, Saturday, each called their parents. Their date was set for two weeks away.

Both families were preparing for the next wedding. Mary's parents had a better income. Mary's dad was bringing home eleven thousand dollars each month. Mary, her mother, Donna, and Karen went shopping for a wedding dress. Mary moved back home until after the wedding. Fred was alone for eleven days. He spent most of those days at his parents' house for company. Fred bought a suit for the wedding.

He was so excited he would sit at the dining table with tears in his eyes. "I wish the wedding would be tomorrow. This waiting is killing me." Everyone laughed. The twins were home also, waiting for Fred's day.

"Just one more week," Jerri said.

"You said that last week." Four days later, they got ready to head to the church, the same one used for Jake's wedding. The wedding ceremonies went great and fast. "I would like you to meet Mr. and Mrs. Fredric Mangrum." The reception was held at the same ballroom. The food was great.

Gary asked, "Girls, all three of you, when are you going to find the right man?"

Mary's younger brother said, "I am still single." Everyone laughed.

After a couple of drinks, Jerri walked over to Tom and looked him eye to eye then grabbed his crotch. He jumped. She said, "What do you have here?"

"I will show you later." He had a deep voice. Tom was only twenty-four. The twins were now thirty and still single. The girls had been looking, but all the men they met were not worth much. After the reception, Jerri took him home. Terri went there also. No more drinks, just a lot of talking then to bed. He satisfied both girls. The next morning, Tom was worn out. The twins were totally happy.

It took Tom a couple of hours to get the strength to make his way to his car and head home. Terri said. "Drive carefully. Come back anytime." There was still a month before school started, so the girls decided to go for a ride on their Can Ams. The trip took them to Peoria. They stopped for lunch then headed home. Terri had to stop for fuel, so Jerri filled her gas tank also.

Now ready to leave, this car pulled in for fuel and stopped in front of the girls. Terri walked to the guys and asked them to move, "and let us go, then you can have the whole area."

"What's wrong? Can't you drive them out, or do you want us to help you?"

Terri said, "I am being nice, boy. Just back up and let my sister and me go. We don't want to hurt you."

The other boy grabbed her arm, Terri hit him four times knocking him out, while Jerri wailed on the other boy. Terri got in their car and backed it up to a parking space. Jerri grabbed one leg of each boy and dragged them over to the front of their car. Terri and Jerri got on their bikes and left. The ladies were looking for the police, but none showed up to stop them.

Neither one said a word about what happened at the gas station. That didn't matter because the station put the video on Facebook. It went national in a heartbeat. Dad called them and talked for a few minutes. The local news ran it also. A news crew came over, but neither girl wanted to talk about what happened.

Jake came over with another police officer, Gary. Jake and the other officer went into their house. The girls explained to them what happened. "We were fine until that guy grabbed my arm. We were just protecting ourselves."

Jake said, "We have watched the video, and we at the station, all agree with your actions."

Gary said, "Don't let your class interrupt you. Tell them schoolwork, children." Jake and Gary left, and the news crew was outside.

Gary said, "The girls were protecting themselves. End of story." The two police walked away. Summer still had another month before school will start.

Terri and Jerri bought a duplex and moved in before school started. Some work was required, so they asked their dad and brothers for some help. Their new home was ready before school started. Their mom came over to help with the decorating. The flooring would come later. Rugs were used to cover the cold floors. Every room had at least one rug. Some were small; others were very large.

Another year of teaching had started for the two women. Their classes wanted to know what happened. Both women had a speech and left it that way. "Now start your schoolwork." The first couple of months were rough on both of them. Moving or changing schools would not help.

Neither one knew what to do.

Jerri called Jake. He came over on the weekend with Dad and Mom and talked for several hours. No solutions were found. Terri said, "I have a solution. I am going to quit teaching. Two and a half months and those kids will not give up." She paused. "I would love to slap the snot out of all those who ask the stupid questions. I will teach until Thanksgiving."

On Monday, Terri went in early and talked to the principal, Allen. When all the classes started, he called a school meeting in the gymnasium. "We have some of the best teachers in the state. Here and in our elementary school next door." A water break. "The problem is we are about to lose two of them after Thanksgiving. These two teachers went for a ride and ended up protecting themselves."

"Now the solution to keep them here is to stop the interrogation period! Any more questions and the two will walk out, never to teach again."

The vice principal said, "You all saw the video. Leave it at that and do your schoolwork." The same message was relayed to the elementary school. Two weeks before the long weekend and things went fair.

The fifth-grade class did not heed the warning. After being in class ten minutes, Jerry dropped the math book on the floor and walked out of the classroom and said goodbye to the principal as she passed the office. She called her sister and said "I quit," then hung up. Jerri went home and fixed a drink.

The principal went to the fifth-grade class and talked to them. He found that two boys would not quit with the questions. He sent them home. He said, "Don't come back until January. Your grades for this time will be a fail." The math book was still on the floor. He picked it up, moved Jerri's chair, and sat down in front of the class. "Miss Mangrum left because she is not able to teach with all those interruptions with questions that are not needed." A pause.

"She will not be back. She quit teaching. She has been teaching nine years now." The principal got up and walked out. He wiped his eyes and went back to the office.

One of the students walked up front and moved the teacher's chair back behind the desk. "When we get back from recess, we will open our English books."

Tommi took over the class until a substitute could be found. Terri continued until Christmas. She also resigned from teaching. Her classes were almost as bad. There were at least two questions each day from one of her classes.

Tony Meek

Born in Idaho in 1940, he grew up fast. His sister Jeana was two years younger. The two were very smart but didn't skip any grades. Elementary school went fast for both children. Their parents, Gene and Sandy, were working full time. Tony and Jeana worked for their clothes during their high school years. Tony made valedictorian of his senior year. With his SAT score, he received a four-year scholarship at Boise State University.

In 1957, he started college. The first year went well. He finished it with a 3.97 GPA. The dean of the school was excited and knew he made a good choice when the staff picked Tony Meek. Boise State was waiting for his sister. Jeana's grades were pretty good but not as high as Tony's grades.

Tony started his second year. Jeana started her senior year of high school. Her grades were falling but still high above the average. She finished high school with 3.68. She didn't want college. Tony attended her graduation. She couldn't afford it. Her parents were not making enough money to help her. Jeana went into the Navy.

After his two college years were complete, Tony decided that he wanted a degree in electrical engineering.

Dad yelled at him, "That profession will never go anywhere!"

"Dad, this is the future of the world. Maybe not this year, but it will grow fast." Tony kept his grades up to the top of the class. Studying hard and lots of rest. He didn't have a girlfriend in college, but in high school, he had his first taste of sex. Jeana finished boot camp and was stationed in San Diego. She went to dispersing school. She finished and advanced to third class, E-4.

Tony could not make it to her boot camp graduation but sent her a letter, saying, "I wish you the best on your future. Be strong and do your best, sis. Love you, Tony." He received her phone number.

He called her. "I have one more year, then I can start my new career in electronics if I can find a job." Tony's last year came to an end with a GPA of 3.97. Before his year ended, a man from General Electric came up to Boise State and talked to him. "Would you like to work for us?" He gave Tony a business card.

Tony said, "I will not waste any more of your time. Yes! Thank you for coming up here to see me."

"We keep a close watch on special students like you. Your pay will be according to your ability. Sixty thousand dollars annually?"

Tony sat down and said, "When do I start?"

"Graduate first, take a week or two off, then come down to San Jose, California. Use the card I gave you. I will be waiting."

"I will be there, Mr. James." The last month of school came to an end and then graduation in 1961. Tony went home and spent a week at home talking to Mom and Dad and his little twin sisters. The two, Joan and Jan, were now in the eighth grade.

Tony said, "Study hard and keep your grades up, girls. I love you both. Mom, Dad, I love you too. I have a job with General Electric in San Jose California. I was told I would start with sixty thousand dollars annually. Is that crazy, Dad? I hope it is that high."

Gene said, "I have looked into electrical engineering. You did pick the right field. I stand corrected, son."

Jeana had advanced to petty officer second class in her first two years. She took leave and visited family and attended Tony's graduation. Jeana was transferred to Moffett Field Naval Air Station six months later. The chief retired. Jeana made first class in November 1961. She was now the division supervisor. Her knowledge of accounting put her up on top of her field. Jeana had one more year to go through to get her bachelor's degree.

Tony held his dad. "I love you, Pop. I have to go to California now." Tony had a flight to San Jose airport. He had two suitcases full of clothes. He saved money from working during the summer and part-time work during the school years. He saved six thousand dollars. His dad received four thousand dollars from Tony before he left to his new job. "I will send you and Mom more when I start work."

Tony started working for GE with good pay. His instructor was Mr. Elmer Mangrum. The two worked together for three years. His learning ability was the highest of any GE first year employee had ever had. Tony was advancing in every category he was assigned to. Tony completed his master's degree in eighteen months.

In November 1963, the president of GE plant called on the intercom, "Attention, all employees." There was a long pause. Tony heard sorrow in his voice. "President Kennedy…has been shot." He started crying. He couldn't say any more. He left for the day.

Tony told Elmer, "He is very upset. We all are. He was a great president."

Elmer said, "He is related to the president. A second cousin." Tony never said another word. President Albertson and family went to DC to be with relatives. The vice president was running GE plant until the president came back. One week passed before Mr. Albertson came back to work. He received several condolences from the employees. They found out several months later, President Kennedy didn't want to have another Korea-style war.

Jeana came to visit Tony at his house. Tony was sending two thousand dollars each month to his parents. He talked to his mom and dad quite frequently. Jeana was now a chief petty officer. A four-year chief.

"Mom, Dad, I am dating a nice man. He is also a chief. We advanced together. He is an aviation machinery repairman. I love him, Mom."

"Has he proposed to you?"

"Not yet, Mom. He will soon. I am sure he will. He says he loves me several time each day. We are living together."

Dad said, "Be careful, honey. I don't want you to have a broken heart. If he breaks your heart, shot him." Then he laughed. "Tony, how are you doing?"

"I am doing fine. I haven't killed anyone yet. I don't have time to be dating a woman. My job keeps me busy."

Jeana said, "I will take care of that, Dad." Tony looked at her. Their talking to their parents ended and hung up the phone. Both of them were back at work now. Three weeks had passed when Jeana called and announced their wedding date.

"Mom, Dad, come down for my wedding please." Tony also talked to his parents. "I will buy your plane tickets. We need you here. We miss your company, Dad and Mom. Bring our sisters. I have a big house here. Five bedrooms. Plenty of room."

Jeana said, "When do you want to leave? Let us know, Dad, Mom."

Dad set a day to depart, and Tony bought four tickets for them. Four days before the wedding, the plane landed at San Jose Airport. Tony picked them up and took them home. The twins were on their last year of high school. The Christmas break was the wedding date of December 28, 1964.

Before the president was killed, Jeana brought a young woman to visit with Tony. He never asked her her age. The two hit it off right away. She was spending all her nights with Tony. Diane was crazy about Tony and likewise. The two were very happy together.

Diane was only a third-class petty officer. Tony didn't know she was only seventeen. He was not interested in her age, just their love for each other. Diane was fixing supper for them. Tony came home and fixed a drink. Diane had the table set.

Tony said, "What is wrong with this setup?" Diane was scared.

Tony went down on one knee and brought a box out of his pocket, opened the box, and asked, "Will you marry me, honey?"

Her reply took less than a second. "Yes!" He stood up and placed the ring on her ring finger. The two held each other with several kisses.

Two days later, he asked, "Dad, Mom, do you want to attend another wedding? Diane is now a second-class petty officer. She works for Jeana in dispersing."

The two set a date for June 21, 1965. The three months went fast. Tony and Jeana went home and attended the twins' graduation.

Diane stayed away for the last four days. Her parents came down for the wedding. Tony gave Diane's parents three thousand dollars for a wedding dress. Diane was now nineteen and very beautiful in her wedding dress. *Is this the same girl?* he thought. Her dad, Jim, walked her up to the altar. Thirty minutes passed, and the priest said, "I am proud to introduce you to Mr. and Mrs. Tony Meek."

A year earlier, Diane said, "My parents are not very rich. That's why I went into the Navy. I will get my degree here."

"I will help you, honey. Jeana says you are doing well." Diane made first class petty officer on March 15. Her uniforms were updated. She was a very happy young lady. Now in her second year in the Navy, she was enjoying married life. She went home after work. "Honey, I have to get a different uniform."

"Why, honey? You look great just like you are."

"I am pregnant, sweetie. Three months."

Tony smiled. "How did that happen?" Then he held her. "Boy or girl?"

"I don't know yet. Another month or so." She called her mom. "Hello, Grandma. Are you ready for a grandchild?"

"Oh my goodness, honey, when?"

"December 15 to 25. I am excited, Mom." The phone call ended. She was back at work the next day. Tony was back working also with a smile on his face.

Elmer asked, "Why the smile, Tony?"

"I will be a father sometime around early December." December came up fast. Diane rode to the hospital in an ambulance. On December 16, 1966, their little girl was born. She was named Heather. Six pounds, seventeen inches.

The big boss came in and got everyone together. "Our boss generator, the one in Saigon, Vietnam, is broken. I need a volunteer." No one wanted to go to the war zone.

"Please, gentlemen."

Tony said, "I will go. The war is up north. I won't be there long." He packed a small bag of clothes.

"No, honey. Please don't go. I need you here."

"Sweetheart, the war is up north. I will be safe in Saigon. Please. I will not be there long." His flight was very long. From San Francisco to Los Angles. Next stop in Hawaii for an hour. A military flight to

Guam, fuel, then Philippines. Another day there, then a flight to Saigon. Tony called while waiting for his flight in the Philippines. He assured her that he would be safe.

It was 1968 in Saigon. Tony got a ride to look at the Boss Generator. Elmer and Tony had designed it, so he knew what he was doing. Tony walked around the generator twice while looking at the manual. He opened a door and reset a switch. The generator lights came on and started up again. Tony called GE and asked for a manual in the Vietnamese language. "These people can speak but cannot read English."

The GE CEO talked to tony. "The generator in Da Nang just quit yesterday. Can you get up there?"

Tony laughed. "Do I have to? Yes, I can get the plane to take me up there." Tony did some shopping with his translator. He saw some used military casings that were made into flower vases. He liked them. He bought eight vases and two lamps made from other material. The items were put on the plane, and they headed for Da Nang.

After getting to the generator, he saw a big mess. Tony spent three days rewiring some parts to make it work right again. The generator was doing its job. His work was finally done. The plane was refueled and would leave in the morning, February 1968. This was the Vietnamese Tet day for celebration. Just before dark, the shooting started. The Tet offensive was in full swing. Every military base in south Vietnam was being attacked.

Tony was outside before the attack started. He headed back in, out of the hail of bullets. Two men fell beside him. He stopped and dragged them inside and went out again. He picked up one of the rifles and shot back at the NVA fighters. Tony knew where the pier was. There were several north Vietnam soldiers trying to steal some boats. Tony shot some of them. The others ran away from that crazy American.

The battle lasted two hours. Tony stayed with the boats. Two Navy men came down to help him guard the boats. When the fighting was over, the sun was down. Tony went to his bed and slept with one eye open. The morning came, and the plane was checked for bullet holes. None were found. The wounded were flown to the hospital ship. The dead men, three, were on the plane with Tony and his translator. The flight to the Philippines was a blessing for Tony. He slept most of the way back to San Francisco.

The crew and Tony were greeted by family members when the plane landed. The three men that died were taken to a funeral parlor.

ZELDA JOAN WILLIAMS

On April 1, 1980, Zelda turned eighteen. She graduated the year earlier from high school. Now out on her own, she still stayed close to home. Her parents were one of the few wealthy Black families in Utah. Though non-Mormon, the family was still well-respected. BYU was a college in the town of Provo, but Zelda didn't want to go to college. Her boyfriend enlisted into the army two years earlier. Zelda wanted to go into the Navy. Her parents said, "If you go against our wishes, you will be stricken from our will."

"I know how many millions you have acquired, and I don't give a damn. If I cannot do what I want, then I will be leaving. I never wanted all that money. All I want is some love from either one of you and never got shit. Give me five minutes to pack some clothes, and I will be out of your hair."

Her mom started crying. "Honey, we have always loved you."

"Mama, I have never seen anything but strict rules. Do this, do that. No 'Thank you,' no 'Good job,' no 'Keep up the good grades,' nothing. I never heard 'Thank you' or 'I love you,' from either one of you. Let me pack some clothes and let me go please." She was crying now.

Her dad came to her, held her, and said, "I am sorry, baby. I guess we forgot the basic things a child loves to hear. It is all my fault. Can you forgive me?"

"I love you, Daddy. Let me live my own life. I don't want to go to any more school right now. I love you too, Mama." She finished packing her suitcase and walked out.

Her mom gave Zelda a thousand dollars. "Be careful, honey. We really do love you."

She got on a bus headed for San Diego. She didn't tell her parents, but she had already enlisted into the Navy. In the naval recruit training center, she was assigned to a company. Two weeks and there were enough recruits to make a company. Zelda was happy for a while until she ran into some very prejudiced people.

She was not the only black person in the company, but those few had to pick on someone. Those few picked the wrong person. Zelda was a third-degree black belt in karate and jujitsu. She had been in the company for three months when these other women decided she was not welcome in the company. Her grades were at the top of the class.

The other women planed a blanket party. Big mistake. The pack of female wolves went to attack her; she was not in her bed. Another woman tipped Zelda off of the planed attack. Those women beat up on several pillows on Zelda's bed. When they realized it, Zelda hit them from the back side, knocking out five of the seven girls. The company commander came yelling at everyone left standing.

When she heard the truth, those seven women were sent back one company. Twelve weeks had ended, and Zelda was advanced to SN (E-3).

Her duty station was at the San Diego naval station. In the personnel office, she learned fast. Then she wanted something different. She checked out the books for dispersing rate. She studied hard and read the book several times.

Zelda had talked to her division officer. "I would like to be a dispersing clerk. What do I need to do to switch?"

He approved her request. He said, "You are a good personnel person, but I will not hold you back." The next test came around, and she took the test. Her score was the top of the test takers. Zelda was advanced to petty officer third class. She did really good in her new field. Six months later, Zelda took the second class test and passed it at the top of the list.

Zelda had the learning ability from her parents. Her mother had a bachelor's degree in teaching, and her father had a master's degree in finance. He knew when to move his money and where to put it. Zelda had saved most of her money and put half in a fidelity account. Now two years in the Navy, she finally wrote a letter home. Her letter was six pages, apologizing for several things and letting them know where she was and what is happening.

Zelda was transferred to a tender. She was happy to get out of San Diego. Put at sea, she was enjoying herself. At twenty, she was feeling the urge for some real love. She didn't like any of the Black men on board the ship. Those men were conceited. Those men thought they were perfect. Some of them smoked dope. She met a White man that was very kind to the people under him. Zelda was one of those. The two talked about anything. She liked Tom but didn't know how to get him interested in her.

Their first stop after Hawaii was the Philippines. She made it known to Tom that she liked him. Tom liked her too but was not supposed to date peers. The two sneaked out on daily off base at liberty. Tom got a room, and the two went out of sight from the rest of the people on the ship.

Tom and Zelda had the weekend off. Love overtook them. Two days of drinking and sex. Monday morning, the two arrived back on board the ship at different times. Tom was five minutes late not to make Zelda late.

He told her, "I can get away with it. You will be grounded for a week." She laughed and walked away and back to the ship five minutes early. Tom was two minutes late.

Every chance the two got while in the Philippines, they would sneak off for a full day together making love. Now back at sea, the ship was headed for Singapore. Singapore was a weird place. Zelda laughed at the wannabe women. "That's not a woman." Its mistake was trying to slap her. This six-foot-two-inch person tried to hit her, at five feet, seven inches. He was too slow. Zelda brought him to his knees with five hits in three seconds. That person lay on the sidewalk in pain.

Two other people approached her, and she and Tom took the offensive. Those guys backed off. Tom took Zelda by the arm and moved her out of that area. After leaving Boogis Street, both of them started laughing. Tom said, "Did you really think you could beat both of them?"

"I had you helping me."

"I don't know a damn thing about karate."

She said, "Oh crap, they would have killed me. I need to train you, baby." Back on board the ship now and safe.

After Singapore, their cruise headed for Kenya. That meant crossing the equator. Neither one had been there before, so both of them were to get their butts beaten. It wasn't all that bad. A little bit of bruising for a few days, then the pain was gone.

They were there for four days. They went off and bought several carved animals then back on the ship. One day off was enough for them. Tom thought that many people knew that he and Zelda were spending time together, but no one said a word.

They stopped at Diego Garcia for three days and did some fishing. From there, the ship was on the way to Australia. There they had a lot of fun. We went to the zoo on the first day and got a room our second day off. They spent most of their time in bed making love. She asked Tom if he wanted to get married.

"No, honey, not while we are on the same ship, baby. I would get reduced in rate and be transferred. We need to stop for the rest of this cruise. Okay, honey?" She agreed. Back on board, the ship cruised around Australia and headed back to the Philippines. We were there a few days then went to Hong Kong for three days. Tom bought several things for his family and got them back on board the ship. Zelda did the same. She bought a place setting of eight china and silverware for her mom and some ivory carvings for her dad.

The ship went back to the Philippines to transfer command. Three days there then the squadron headed home to San Diego. Tom Davis was called into the division officers' office. "Petty Officer Davis, you came on board five years ago as an E-3. You went all the way up to become division petty officer. Where do you want to go?"

"I don't really know, sir. I would like to get shore duty somewhere if I can't stay here."

"Well, I have to transfer you. I don't have room for two chiefs." Tom's eyes lit up. He made chief. "Who is replacing me? Do you have a first class coming on board?"

"No, she is already on board. Petty Officer First Class Zelda Williams will take your position. Tell her I want to see her."

Tom went to his desk and looked at Zelda. He said, "Petty Officer Williams, the division officer wants to talk to you." She got up and walked to his office. She was scared that he found out that she and Tom had been making love. When Zelda left, Tom let out a silent yell.

Zelda arrived at the division officers' office. She knocked and walked in. "Have a seat, Petty Officer. I am having to transfer Petty Officer Davis." She thought she would be transferred also.

"Tom made chief petty officer. You will be taking his job, Petty Officer First Class Williams." He was smiling now. Zelda breathed a sigh of relief and smiled as she thought what she would do now.

The DO asked, "Do you think you can handle the job?"

"Yes, sir. I am ready."

"I didn't mean to scare you, P. O. Williams. Chief Davis already knows. I talked to him earlier." A pause. "Go tell him, get out of my desk." Then he laughed. Zelda also laughed. She looked at her left arm. She went out and walked to Tom. "Petty Officer Davis, get away from my desk." Both of them laughed.

"Yes, ma'am," then he held her. "I am going to shore duty. I haven't decided where yet."

Tom went through his chief's initiation in Hawaii. Zelda had the division PO desk and updated her uniform to first class. She was twenty-one now and had only one more year to complete her four-year enlistment.

Tom put on his chief's uniform when the ship got back to San Diego. He was given a temporary bunk in the chief's quarters.

Tom wanted shore duty in San Diego. He was sent to NAS Lemoore in central California. He and Zelda would talk twice a week. Zelda and Tom were missing each other. She said, "Only four more months, honey." She was going to get out of the Navy, then he could marry her. The last four months were very slow, but finally, she walked off the ship and headed for Lemoore NAS.

She had sold all her leave because she would not go back into the Navy. Zelda arrived at the naval base. She called Tom. He went out to greet her with open arms. The two held each other.

He said, "That was the longest year of my life."

She said, "Me too, sweetie."

"I have a house out in town." She was tired from driving. Tom took her home and went back to work. He was excited to have her there. The work day was just about done. Tom left five minutes early with the DOs, okay to go. He got home and found Zelda still sleeping. He went in and kissed her cheek then went to the kitchen.

He thought, *What shall I fix for supper? I will be cooking for two,* as he smiled. He was looking in the freezer when Zelda got up and went into the kitchen to greet Tom again.

She said, "I would like to cook up some chicken for supper." He said okay. Tom opened the freezer and brought out a half chicken. She took the chicken and turned on the stove.

Zelda said, "That was easy. Now all I have to do is clean the food off the plates."

Tom said, "No, I want you to wash them before you put them in the dishwasher." Then he laughed. Tom cleaned the table and put the dishes into the dishwasher, added soap, closed the door, and then turned it on.

"But—" Tom then started laughing.

Zelda hit him lightly. "You brat."

"Honey, is it alright if I stay in the Navy and retire?"

"Baby, I have to think about that. Give me some time please."

One week, he came home, and she just finished cleaning the whole house.

Tom looked around and said, "Did you take a break from all the cleaning? I hope."

"Yes, I did. I took a minute to pee." She laughed. "Did you ever clean this house?"

"Yes, honey. I vacuumed once a week each month."

She laughed again and shook her head. "Oh my God."

Tom went down on one knee and said, "I am sorry. Will you forgive me?" Then he reached into his pocket and brought out a small box, opened it, and said, "Will you be my wife and marry me?"

Zelda started crying and said, "Yes, sweetie." Tom stood up and placed the ring on her finger. Tom held her and received several kisses from Zelda. A week later, the wedding date was set for August 1.

Zelda called her parents to let them know she was about to change her name. Tom called his parents and told them his plans to get married. He gave them the date. Tom's parents were living in St. George, Utah.

Her mom asked, "Is he a nice man? Will he treat you right and not beat on you?"

"Mom, we love each other. Yes to all your questions. He is a chief in the Navy. He wants to stay and retire from the Navy. I said yes. Our wedding day is the first day of August this year." Three days later, her parents arrived at Lemoore Naval Air Station. Her father called Zelda. She arrived at the gate. He followed her home. Her parents drove down from Provo, Utah.

Her dad, Tyrone, asked, "Why are you living off base?"

"Tom doesn't like the bachelor's quarters. He said there isn't enough room to move around. Most of the chiefs and some officers live off base. I spent three years working for him. We fell in love, and I spent my last year alone. It just made our love for each other to grow."

Her mom said, "When does he get home? Soon I hope."

"Mom, Dad, he is a White man. Is that a problem?"

Her dad quickly replied, "No, not at all." Tom made it home early. He left work when Zelda called.

"Mr. and Mrs. Williams, I finally get to meet you. I am Thomas Davis."

The four talked for several hours. Zelda and Joan fixed supper. Tom went to work in the morning. Zelda set them up in a motel close to their house. Tom got a call from his mom. His parents were in town. He went to the gate and put them up in the hotel on base for the day. He said, "I have one more hour then I will take you to the motel close to my house."

Tom got off work, and his parents followed him home. At home, Zelda was there. His father said, "Oh my god, she is beautiful. Where did you find her?" He could see the Negro ancestry.

Tom said, "We worked together for three years on the tender. We fell in love there. Now we want to get married." Her parents came over. Tom introduced the parents of both families.

Tyrone said, "We spent a lot of time in the sun." Everyone laughed.

Marci said, "I hate the sun." More laughter.

Tom Senior. asked, "Do you snow ski?"

Tyrone said, "If there aren't four tires under me, then I don't feel safe."

His wife, Joan, said, "Quit lying. Yes, we do ski. Utah has several nice ski parks. Sometimes we go to northern Utah to try out their slopes."

Zelda said, "Supper will be done in a few minutes. Everyone, have a seat. What do you want to drink? Water, milk, beer, or wine?"

Tyrone said, "No bourbon?" Then he laughed.

They had steak for supper. Everyone got stuffed. They talked through supper and several hours after. Tom had reserved a room for his parents at the motel across the street from his house. The room was next to Zelda's parents' room. Everyone sat outside their rooms and talked for an hour and had a couple of drinks of bourbon and water. Tom Junior and Zelda went home and went to bed.

Tom went to work in the morning and requested two weeks' leave. He was given ten days starting Monday. Twelve days off. Tom worked two more days then was off the weekend and ten more days off. That time covered August first, plus three days. Joan put Zelda up in a motel room, and Tom wanted to move his parents into his spare room. His dad said, "No. We will stay here. We like this room." The wedding was set with the base chaplain.

Tom Senior had met Tyrone once several years earlier. He never said anything, but he knew the Williamses were very wealthy. Before the wedding, Tyrone talked to Tom Senior and his wife. "What does he know about me?"

"I don't know," Marci said.

Tom asked, "Zelda, what did you tell our son? I...we...met your parents many years ago. We know what your parents are worth. If he is marrying you for money, I will not approve it."

"He knows I am single and in love with him. As for my parents' money, nothing that I know of."

Tom Junior went over to the motel and asked, "Mr. Williams, do you need some extra money for Zelda's wedding dress? I can help with six hundred dollars."

His dad and mom went to his house and set down and talked to Junior for several hours. "That was very nice to offer the extra money. They will need it. Why did you offer the money, son?"

"Black families don't have much money. If my funds will help, then I will be happy for the Williams family."

His mother, Marci, asked, "What do you know about her parents?"

"They are dark-skinned. Darker than Zelda. But she told me that she was Black when we first met, but I already knew that. What else should I know? Did he spend time in prison?"

Senior laughed. "No, son. Don't worry about it. Just enjoy your marriage and stay nice to her."

"I will, Dad. Always. I love her very much, and I am sure she loves me just as much."

Mom asked, "Is there anything left to drink?" Junior looked at his watch.

"The store is still open. What do you want to drink?" Tom drove to the base exchange and took them shopping.

"Take some to Zelda's parents."

"Thank you, son." Tom Senior took some drinks to Tyrone and Joan. Tom and his parents had a drink and talked for a while longer then went home for the night. Two more days, then he got dressed for the wedding.

Tom was waiting by the priest when Zelda and her father walked up to the front next to the priest. She looked beautiful in her wedding dress. Tom didn't know what to think. The priest said a few words that Tom didn't hear. He was looking at Zelda. "Tom, did you hear what I said?"

"Yes, I do." The priest just smiled. Tom placed the ring on her finger.

The priest said the vows again, and Zelda placed the ring on Tom's finger. "You may now kiss the bride. I would like you to meet Mr. and Mrs. Tomas Davis Jr. The reception was at the chief's club." Part of the wedding party was several chiefs and wives. Two hours there, and Tom and Zelda left for home. Their parents left also. Three days left of leave then back to work. His last day, both families got together for dinner and a few drinks.

Tom was back to work now. He had two new women working for him that were not doing very well. He got angry but controlled his temper. Tom talked to the DO about these two women's ability. "The women need help. I know my wife can help them. She left the Navy after her four-year enlistment as a very intelligent first class."

"We can't pay her, Chief Davis."

"I know that, but those two women need some help. I will talk to my wife tonight." Tom talked to Zelda that evening. She said she would try to help them. Tom had seven people working under him. Four were women. Zelda went to work with Tom the next day. She met Tom's boss. He talked to her for a few minutes and found that she still had her secret security clearance. Zelda went to the dispersing office with Tom.

"This is my wife, Zelda. She has more patience than I do. Jeanni and Clair, come here." Zelda had a talk with them and a few lessons on dispersing and bookkeeping. Both girls were SN E-3. Zelda asked them to get the third class book and read it. When you had read it, then you could help yourself. Both girls did much better after reading the book. Tom was happier now and could trust them to do a better job.

Zelda took classes to get a finance degree. She would go to Fresno college and take a test once a week. Her reading assignment was done at home. Three semesters done and she received her bachelor's degree. With her Navy training, she completed the degree early. Tom went with her to witness the occasion. Tom filmed her walk for her finance, bookkeeping bachelor's degree.

About the Author

Robert was born in Idaho in 1944. In 1951, he started school in Charleston, Oregon. He finished the first grade. In 1954, the family moved to Waldport, Oregon. There he finished most of his education.

Robert's family moved again to Northbend, Oregon, where he finished his junior year. When he turned eighteen, he went into the Navy. He loved the travel to other countries. Twenty-two years later, he retired from the Navy. He then started working for civil service as a machinist. The Navy must have liked his work because he was selected for the Civilian Employee of the Month twice, and once for Civilian Employee of the Year. His first seven years in the civil service were at Moffett Field Naval Air Station with the regular Navy. The regular Navy moved to Texas. NASA owns Moffett Field now. The reserve Navy moved to Moffett Field. Five years later, the reserve Navy moved to Southern California. Robert found a job at Hill Air Force Base in Utah. He finished his time there and retired with twenty-two years of civil service. He is now fully retired. He moved to Missouri and stayed with his brother until he found his own place in a very nice quiet town with a population of 665. He has lived alone since retirement. He enjoys fishing, especially fly-fishing. Things are slow in this small town, so he takes long walks around town. He visits his oldest daughter and oldest brother. Both of them live not far away from him. Robert was not very interested in history in school. Now he loves reading about it. He has lived for seventy-three years and plans for another twenty-five years.

Lightning Source UK Ltd.
Milton Keynes UK
UKHW011045050821
388368UK00001B/91